Sins of a Thug

Sins of a Thug

**Lock Down Publications and Ca$h
Presents**

Sins of a Thug
A Novel by *Monet Dragun*

Lock Down Publications
P.O. Box 944
Stockbridge, Ga 30281

Visit our website @
www.lockdownpublications.com

Copyright 2020 Monet Dragun
Sins of a Thug

First Edition November 2020
Printed in the United States of America

This is a work of fiction. Names, characters, places, and incidents either are products of the author's imagination or are used fictitiously. Any similarity to actual events or locales or persons, living or dead, is entirely coincidental.

Lock Down Publications
Like our page on Facebook: Lock Down Publications @
www.facebook.com/lockdownpublications.ldp
Cover design and layout by: **Dynasty Cover Me**
Book interior design by: **Shawn Walker**
Edited by**: Leondra Williams**

Stay Connected with Us!

Text **LOCKDOWN** to 22828 to stay up-to-date
with new releases, sneak peaks, contests and
more…
Thank you.

Submission Guideline.

Submit the first three chapters of your completed manuscript to ldpsubmissions@gmail.com, subject line: Your book's title. The manuscript must be in a .doc file and sent as an attachment. Document should be in Times New Roman, double spaced and in size 12 font. Also, provide your synopsis and full contact information. If sending multiple submissions, they must each be in a separate email.

Have a story but no way to send it electronically? You can still submit to LDP/Ca$h Presents. Send in the first three chapters, written or typed, of your completed manuscript to:

LDP: Submissions Dept
P.O. Box 944
Stockbridge, Ga 30281

DO NOT send original manuscript. Must be a duplicate.

Provide your synopsis and a cover letter containing your full contact information.

Thanks for considering LDP and Ca$h Presents.

Monet Dragun

Prologue

This shit is not for the kindhearted.
That good boy exterior; that ain't me.

I was always told to be someone I wasn't, to live up to my younger brother's expectations. Ain't that bout a bitch? *My younger brother!* Well, football was my life; and I use that term lively. It was my ticket away from my father's money and criticism.

I was only going to play football to please my father: The Preacher. The man who could do no wrong, who was flawless. But I knew all too well that was a lie. My mother, now she was a real Saint. God bless her soul, and may she rest in peace. I loved her more than anything, but she died from a broken heart. My father wasn't all that faithful and that happens with a lot of pastors and beyond. But the hypocrite that he is, he'll never own up to his wrongdoings. He's a son of the Lord.

My brother was the so-called angel. He ain't none of that. Far from the bullshit. He copied off everything that I did, which was one reason why I quit football altogether. My one and only passion flushed down the drain. I could never have something of my own. Nothing to my name. Even though he sucked at the sport, he still managed to make varsity. Go figure, right? Even though I was the oldest, I was second best. Ain't that some bullshit at its best?

My momma always said, don't let no one change you, make them take you as you are. And I took heed to that. Plus, my father has his own secrets. There's a difference between a father and a dad. I learned that at an early age.

***

I pulled into the Gentleman's Club and cut off my Escalade before hopping out. I put on my shades and walked into the business. I was greeted by all the women workers in a matter of seconds. I said my hello's and skipped up the steps to my office.

I went to open the door only for a shortframed girl to pull the door. She smiled at me and walked straight past me as if nothing happened at all. She fixed herself and made her way down the steps. All I could do was shake my head. I knew my business partner. My best friend was up to no damn good. But, in my office? One of my ladies just gave him some top. I knew this scene all too well. She'll be fired for fraternizing. "Sup, Marcus. But get ya' ass up out my seat." He nodded as I strolled into the office.

"Wuzzam, she's a keeper right' there." I shook my head and took a seat in my chair. I took my shades off and laid them on my desk as he sat down across from me. He was skimming over some shit.

"She'll be gon' by the morning," I mumbled.

Marcus caught my attention. "Aye, Troy we made all the drops and I 'ma need some more for the boys." I nodded.

"How much?" I questioned.

"Bout' twenty of em." I nodded once again and went to my desk handing him two black duffel bags.

"I'll get back to you lata'." He grabbed the bags, I dapped him up as he got up from the chair then he walked towards the door. My phone buzzed making me look at it.

My Queen: Papi, when you coming home? I miss you. *sent now.*

I chuckled at her message and quickly replied. She was always worried bout' me and this business.

Me: Guh, I gotta work today you know that. *Read.*

She hates when I tell her no, and with the work I do, I know I won't be getting any. I'm so not in the mood for one of her fits right about now. A few minutes later, my phone buzzed again. I picked it up looking at it and signed. This girl just couldn't keep her hands off me.

My Queen: You just have gone leave me all hot and bothered like this?

Her message came in immediately and I smirked as I replied.

Me: Betta' stop playing with me! You know I gave you some this morning. I'ma be home tonight. *Read.*

Me: I'll be home at 5. You betta stay just like that too. And don't think you gone run tonight.

I sent the message to her phone, then put my phone on the desk. My nigga Mega came in and I nodded for him to sit down. Before, I could say anything, my iPhone began to ring. I held up my finger to signal him to hold on.

"One the minute it's the wifey." He nodded and sat down in the leather seat. "Hello." My ears were met with the love sounds of Alexus. "Why are you playing with me, man? I'ma tear dat' ass up for this. I swear fo' God, Lex."

"Oh, Papi I want you to!" Mega broke out laughing. I pulled the phone away and looked at him. He straightened his face. I shook my head and put the phone back to my ear. To hear her moaning my name so good, it made my manhood twitch.

"That's it, I'll be there soon."

"Adios Papi." I shook my head at her antics and hung up.

"Boss, I 'ma handle this." I nodded.

"Alright, I'll be back lata' on tonight' I gotta handle the wifey." He smirked and dapped me up. Grabbing my shades off the desk, I made my way out of my office. Mega walked out of my office and locked it behind him.

Making it outside, I started up and backed up out of my parking spot and was back on the road to my crib. She gon' get enough for fucking with me when I'm on the job.

But you never thought the Preachers son would be doing this for a living huh?

Monet Dragun

Chapter One

Alexus fixed my tie for me as she dusted my shoulders off. She stepped off the stool as I stood in the fulllength mirror examining myself. "Damn, I look good," I said sounding all cocky after licking my lips.

She rolled her eyes and giggled a bit. "You are so damn cocky. But mph you fine, Papi." She said while walking towards her vanity as she smoothed out her dress. She was so beautiful. It was a shame. She fluffed her curls as I slowly took all her features in. "Why are you looking at me that way?" She probed.

"Damn I can't look at you now and No reason. I just got a sexy girlfriend that's been down for me," I said walking towards her, bending down and wrapping my long, lanky arms around her slim waist. I kissed her cheek a few times before looking at both our reflections in the mirror.

"You know I got you. But you don't have to go to this dinner if you don't want to, babe. I know how you and your father can get." She said, as I deeply sighed and pulled away from her.

"It's a family dinner. *My* momma would at least want me to try. I don't want her turning in her grave over me and my father's bickering. I'm trying. I'm trying for her. You know I made her a promise, Lex." She sighed and turned to face me.

"I know, but darling look. Every time you go near that place, your brother tries to break you down and do anything he can for your father to snap on you. Besides, being that your brother's girlfriend just had a baby, maybe he'll leave you alone." She said with all honesty.

I ran my hand down my freshly shaved face and fiddled with my chin hairs. "Well, one day or another, it is going to come out that I'm a thug and a drug dealer. I know I'ma big disappointment to my father, but I'm not about to kiss his ass, or make him proud. I'm not seventeen and in high school anymore. I learned to not let his antics go after my momma passed away." She sighed and blinked twice.

"Love, I know that, and you are not a damn drug dealer. There's a difference between a thug and a drug dealer. So, stop calling yourself that. I'm glad you are trying, but please for me, don't blow up at this dinner, Troy. I know you. One thing said that doesn't sit well with you about your lifestyle and you'll explode. You know you can be petty at times. You'll spill all the secrets and tea your damn self at any rip." I nodded and put my hand in my left pocket as I looked at the time on my phone.

"I won't be petty this time. Now, come on. You don't need all that makeup on anyway, beautiful." She smiled that sweet smile and it always made me melt.

I held out my hand and she took it as we walked out of the room. I prayed to any God that this dinner will go right. Momma helps me.

We walked out to the S500 Mercedes truck and I helped her in. She pulled her red velvet dress in so it wouldn't get closed in the door on her side. As I walked over to my side of the truck, my phone started to buzz. Pulling it out, I looked at it, and it was my brother. Speak of the damn devil. I was not about to rush just to get to this dinner. I know it was to see my first niece. But I know his smart mouth ass gone say something. So, I decided to decline the call.

I hopped in the car and put the key in, starting up the truck and backing out of our short driveway. "Babe, who called?" Lex questioned.

"Just my bruh, that's all." The look on my face gave her a true answer. She just leaned over and pecked me on the cheek.

"Relax, the dinner will go fine, love." I sighed. I knew, I just knew all too well that this dinner was going to be full of bullshit. I needed a bullshit button just to pull me out of the bullshit.

***

Here comes the bullshit. I already knew this dinner was going to be a disaster. I still had the gut feeling, just cause my girl told me to relax. I just couldn't do that. We held hands as we stood on the doorstep. If only I could just attend this shit, maintain my composure and leave this entire event with my girl, so we can have a peaceful night. Never again would I ever come to this house. It ain't gone happen. My palms began to sweat. This could either go wrong or go right. More than likely it will go wrong. I just wanted to have a great dinner and leave. No bullshit, no fighting, just having a cordial feast with my family. Lex gripped my hand tighter, trying her best to soothe me.

"Baby, relax. I can tell when you're stressing. Just stay calm. Everything will be fine." Lex reassured. I smiled as I hesitated to knock on the door. I haven't been to my father's house in I don't know how long and for good reasons.

My heart began to thump rapidly in anxiety. Remembering what Lex said and the little memo or pep talk I had with myself. Let's get in, eat dinner, put a smile on or face, and then leave.

Lex pulled me out of my thought when she rang the doorbell and waited for a response. She rubbed my cheek with her smooth and soft warm hands, made my heart slow it's beat down.

"Who is it?!" The person on the opposing end yelled.

"It's Troy and Lex," I responded in a deep voice. Heavy footsteps thumped towards the door and eventually swung it open. I was now faced to face with the man who I didn't want to see. My father.

"Hello. Hello nice seeing you here. It's been ages, don't you say." My father joked, but I found nothing humorous about this situation. I gave him a weak smile and walked into the house with Lex in tow. "Hol' up now. You speak when you enter this house. I know you ain't bout walk past me in my home and not greet me. Don't make me get my holy water." My father scolded. He embraced me into a tight hug. But I didn't want him touching me. I looked over my father's shoulder to see Lex glancing at me uncomfortably. I rolled my eyes and hugged him in return.

"Hello Father." I mustered to say. When he let me go, we made brief eye contact. He broke it and looked at Lex, acting as if seeing her was brand new.

"And look here. Your beautiful girlfriend, Alexus. I can't believe my son got himself such a masterpiece. Welcome to my home, baby girl." He greeted, kissing her hand. She blushed oh this shit was too much.

"Father, you've known her since we were in high school," I said walking into the dining room to see the dinner table was set with plates, forks, and knives. No food was laid out yet. I'm sure it was only cause Prince Charming wasn't here yet. Typical.

Well, at least he decided to do something exceptionally right I snarled mentally. Lex gave me a look and I composed myself from being petty. I pulled a chair for Lex. She sat down and I pushed it in for her, taking a seat next to her.

"Thank you, baby," Lex said, puckering her lips. I leaned in and kissed her lips.

"You're welcome. You know I love you." I replied. She giggled that little laugh I loved so much, and I grinned.

"Your brother said he's on his way." My father announced.

"Okay," I replied, sarcastically. Lex nudged me in the stomach hard reminding me to remain cordial. Groaning lightly, I eyed her with a slight smile. This woman always kept me in check when need be. "Alright. I'm so excited to see him, Ciara, and the baby." I corrected it. Lex smiled, approving my statement. A tall, light brown skin woman, with long black hair, came into the room making her presence known. My father pulled her into a hug and kissed her sweetly. I know he didn't go marry off. No one can replace my momma.

"Hello, you must be Troy. I've heard a lot about you." She smiled, but I knew my father ain't talk about me. More like she heard little of me.

"Nice meeting you and you are?" I said giving her a small hug as she came around the table.

"I'm Melina. I'm your father's wife." She smiled. Go figure lady.

I was about to say something when the door opened, and my brother strolled in like he was the shit, with Ciara trailing right behind him with the newborn in her arms.

"Hey, all." He greeted. Then he glanced at me with and with a kiss of his teeth, "Troy."

"Stephen." I grabbed the glass of water and sipped before I said anything disrespectful. Now I really see that this dinner is going to be hell. Everyone hugged one another and I held my little niece for the first time. She was so beautiful, looked nothing like Stephen. Thank God.

Soon the rest of them were seated, with one clap from my standing father the food came rolling in. Soon taking a seat, Stephen wasted no time with his bullshit.

"So, Troy?" He said looking at me as the servers brought in the food. I knew this wasn't all my father's work.

"Sup?" I said as everyone was about to start eating. And having nice conversations.

"How's your line of work going for you?" I put my fork down and looked him dead in the eyes.

"Why does it matter to you, Stephen?", I said getting angry by the second. Cause it's always him that starts the bull, and I wasn't up for it not at all. Alexus paused as she touched my wrist but glared at Stephen at the same time.

"Yeah, son, what do you do? You quit football, so I hope God put you in the right path and you know, not a bum."

"Curtis!" Melina said slapping him on the arm.

"No, I'm not a bum and don't worry about what I do. Does it look like I'ma bum? The way I and my girl are dressed?" My father shrugged. This was making me sick.

"You call hanging your pants halfway off your behinds dressed? You know I taught you better than that." My father said sharply.

"I heard he is slangin'," My brother said with a snicker. The whole room got quiet. My father dropped his fork and looked at me.

"Is that true?!" he shouted. His deep voice fazed me none.

"And again why does it matter? I don't give a damn what you think. I stopped that a long time ago." He stood up from his seat and pointed his finger at me making everyone flinch, except me.

"You will not talk like that in my house or at me! This is the Lord's hou"

"You're nothing but a damn hypocrite! That's why moms gone today! You were probably cheating on her with this lady. Mom died a year a fuckin' go and you got a wife that fast? And the Lord has blessed my heart. I'm not sure I can say the same about you. I don't care if I'm a son of a preacher! You have hated me, not cared for me and, you've called call me a disappointment all my life and you always kissed his ass. Me, the family fuck up. I don't need you and I never will need you. My momma told me to be myself and don't change for no one else. And, to make you feel good, I'm a thug. How you like that Curtis? Come on Lex, let's go. I'm not hungry anymore. Ciara, I'll send you a gift for the baby. Love you, and Stephen, go fuck yourself, 'cause you ain't shit but a carbon copy of me." I grabbed Lex's hand as we stalked towards the door.

"TROY! TROY GRIFFIN! Don't you walk out that got'damn door!" Everyone looked at him. I knew he would show his true self.

"Watch me!" I opened the door and I and Lex left. I've been wanting to get that off my chest for a long time. And I'm glad I did. I knew Lex was going to give me the third degree. The whole "you should have handled that better" thing, but he they needed to hear all of that. And that's the honest God truth, I knew the Lord loved me. But, my father, I could give a rat's ass about.

Chapter Two
Troy

"Bottles on me!" I said as I sat in my VIP section. The crowd at my Gentleman's club was outrageous. The girls were wild, and the players were out. The women spun on the pole like it was their last chance. They dipped to keep the women pleased. Twerked so hard, you'd thought they would break their backs for that cash for the men and even women throwing ones.

"Aye, T is that Lex over there?" My eyes lit up to see my girl. She was accompanied by a couple of her homegirls, but when my eyes landed on her, some nigga was all in her space, and once her hand went in his face, she tried to walk away, and he grabbed her, I snapped. I don't play them games. He knows where the fuck he at?

"Fuck, type of shit is that? Niggas know I don't play 'bout mine!" I said getting heated.

"Mane, she ain't got no interest in him. He is touching the wrong Sis. He all up on ha'. Thirsty as hell!" I took a swig of my Gin and juice and sat my glass down as I made my way down the steps. Everyone cleared me a path when they seen my face.

"Aye, Lil mama fuck yo' man. I can do ya' phat booty ass betta' and treat fat ma even betta'," He slurred as she pulled away from him, disgusted as he spoke some reckless shit with spit flying out of his mouth like he had no sense. He nearly made her drink spill all over the dress I bought. But he quickly slapped her ass. Very damn disrespectful. Lexus grabbed her drink or whoever drink it was and threw it in his face.

"Nigga don't you ever put your grimy ass hands on me! You don't know me. My boyfriend gon' come down hea' and whup yo' bitch ass!" He got more aggressive and that's when I stepped in.

"Yo'! You disrespecting my guh'? In my place? Nigga yo' ass will be buried up to your neck in dirt with a water hose down your throat if keep fuckin' with mine! Aye, Tony! Escort this bitch ass nigga out, before the police get called up here and I be in jail." He was silent and didn't say a word to me. I run this shit. He should've known better.

"A'ight, boss! Nigga you either walk or get ya' ass dragged out for touchin' on the misses." He shrugged.

"Mane, I ain't scared of this broad, nigga!" He pulled out a baby ass bitch pistol and pointed it in my face. It ain't faze me none. The music scraped and it was dead silent.

"Nigga, you sho' you wanna pull that?" I stepped forward. "You should look around. I got guns pointed at ya' ass right now." His hand started to shake, and I grabbed the gun flipping it on him and pointed it in his face. "Now what's good?" He put his hands up and Tony grabbed him dragging him out.

"We good peeps. Back to the party!" And when the beat dropped, they did just that.

Lex looked up at me. "Baby, me and the girls was trying to get up to the section when that bum ran all up on me!" I grabbed Alexus by her waist and pulled her close to me, making her grin uncontrollably.

"It ain't no thang ma'. I know you would never do me like that." She pecked my lips softly. I looked her up and down as all her curves showed through her leather dress. "I should beat yo' ass for what you got on. I don't give a damn if I bought it. But you know daddy will let you slide this one time." She giggled and turned her back as her pressed her body against my front.

"You bought it for me though! But how are you feeling? You know about the dinner last night and all?" Running my hand down my face, I sighed with frustration. Even though I didn't give a damn what my father thought, it still kind of stung that he could care less about me. "Troy?" She said over the music.

"I'm good babe, I'm good. Let's just have fun tonight, alright? Enjoy the opening of my new club. Okay?" I kissed her on the top of the head, and she danced against me. Then I whispered, "Aye, I bought this dress for my eyesonly, mamas." She giggled as Lex ass swayed in a circular eight motion. As the DJ changed the song to Rico Love's, *They Don't Know,* Lexus began to snap her fingers and really grind on me. I couldn't help but hold her hips and move with her.

Knowing damn well she was tipsy, I bent my head down to her level, I whispered into her ear. "When we get home, I'ma give you what you are asking for." She smacked her teeth in a playful manner and continued to dance on me. Hearing a whistling tone, I looked up at one of my boys as he waved me over to the section. "Babe, I'll be back. Stay with T and girls." She nodded and continued to dance and sip the little liquor she had left in her cup. I made my way through the crowd and to the section, where Don had been at whole time with some girls.

"Sup, man?" I said dapping him up. He moved the girls off him and looked at me.

"Did you ever know we was going to come up like this?" He questioned. I chuckled and leaned back in my seat a little. Like for real my mans. Save the emotional talk for another time.

"Nah, I didn't. We used to be good boys. What happened?" I smirked and we both broke out laughing.

"We grew out of that shit. That's what happened." He said feeling on one of the ladies beside him. I shook my head and got up.

"Gotta make it rain on my people." He nodded and shooed me off. One day his ass gone get caught up or even catch something. Going down the steps, I looked at what all I built, what I helped to establish. I walked down the side path on the second floor and made my way to the DJ Booth. He gave me a head nod and I grabbed the mic.

"How everybody doing tonight'?" The whole club went into a roar of screams and indistinctive words. I chuckled and looked at the DJ. "You ready bro?" He asked.

"More than!" I hit the green button and money rained down from the ceiling. "Tell em' ya boy Trojan the shit!" The DJ changed the song to Tory Lanez *Say It*. I made my way back to Lexus. She had the most lustful look on her face. Running my hand down her bare shoulder, I bit my lip as Lex ran her hand down my chest and grabbed the rim of my jeans, making me smirk. I said, "Bae, are you drunk girl?" She shrugged.

"I may be a little tipsy, Troy. When you gone put the Trojan on for me?" She smirked. I broke out in laughter. She was a mess when she was drunk.

"Girl, I'm working with this Hennessy dick. You know we don't use those. My pull-out game is too strong." She bit her lip, and I pecked her lips.

"Then let's get out of here, so you can get me out of this!" She whined. I shook my head and pulled her close to me as she slow danced against my member. She knew exactly what she was doing, and I had to get her ass out of here soon before she ended up pulling me into one of the bathrooms.

***

Massaging my hands on her lower back, Alexus' giggled as I slipped my tongue into her mouth. Loving the taste of that sweet lip stick she wears so much. Lexus wrapped her legs around me as we entered our bedroom. Roughly pulling each other's clothes off, she kissed all up on my neck something serious. I laid her on the bed and kissed all down her neck and chest. Pulling her dress top down, I took my hands and ripped her bra in half. "Oh, Troy! You better not tease me!" She whined.

"Where the fun in that if I can't see you shiver under my touch." I lifted my head and kissed her stomach and went up to her left breast as I kissed, licked, and sucked on them. Even palming the right one. And indeed, she shuddered under my touch. "See what I mean?" I toyed.

"Troy, stop playing!" She said leaning up and kissing me then kissing down to my jimmy. She began unbuckling my jeans. "I want you and I want you now, Papi!" That liquor had her way beyond freaky.

"Damn mama, yo" I was cut off when her mouth was on my member. This was one of the reasons I loved her. She was a big ass freak, and she didn't give a fuck about it either. "Lexus, baby you are doing some magic." I groaned. I ran my hand through her brownblonde hair, and she went deeper, doing the shit I loved. She did that trick with her tongue where she made her throat flex like a fucking pro.

"Just like that baby." I bit my lip trying not to give into her so quickly. But the way she was handling me, I knew I would. She gently pulled me out of her mouth and smirked. She stroked me up and down, twisting tightly, making my eyes go low with lust. I pushed her back on the bed and pulled her dress completely off.

"You think you gone make me bust that quick?" I asked her. She bit her lip as my tongue snakes around the string of her thong, "And who told you to walk out of this house with this on, huh?" I questioned as I pulled it down with my teeth.

"I could've been a bad girl and not worn any panties under this at all." She giggled. I just straight faced her and slapped her thigh and pulled her down to the edge of the bed by her thighs. Grasping her thick thighs, I pushed them apart. Eyeing her juicy pussy like it was my last meal, I startled her by holding her thighs down, diving my head in licking all around her clit, sending her into loud cries and moans.

Lex tried to escape my hold. She tried to back away from my begging tongue that was lapping away at her juices.

"Say some smart shit again!" I said making her grab my hair.

"Baby, I'm sorry. Oh, my fuck! Yes!" My phone started to buzz, and I rolled my eyes. "Let it ring baby please, I'm close! You know damn well yyou are licking on my spot baby!" She moaned, I absolutely hated to stop. But my phone wouldn't let up.

"Just hold it for me and lemme get this." I heard her smack her lips. As I felt her pour pussy pulsating. I looked up and she was giving me that face that made me give into her, "Just a second babe. Just a second." She rolled her eyes as I moved away from her body. Picking up my phone. Just staring at the screen as the words—

Stephen is calling.

Rolled across the screen.

"The fuck?" Seriously debating if I should even answer it.

"Answer it since you made me fucking wait. Got me all damn hot and bothered and shit. Fucking wet as fuck and you wanna answer a damn phone." Lexus sasses. I knew she drunk and mad. I'ma just fuck her up the right way for talking back to me.

So, I did what she said. And answered the phone. "Wuzzam'in?" I said blandly into the phone.

"Bro, I know we have our differences, but I'm in a bind. I want in." I knitted my eyebrows together.

"Come again? Into what? What do you mean exactly?" I questioned.

"Into your drug business. I need fast money. Please, just help me out." I looked at Lexus. She got up from the bed as her bare ass swayed back and forth. I was kind of distracted until I heard him calling my name.

"My bad, but Stephen you can't get into this. This ain't ya' lifestyle. Stick with football man." I said running my hand down my face. Trying to stop myself from laughing.

"That's the thing ththey kicked me off the team for doing steroids. I won't be able to get back on the team." Inside I was like nigga that's what you get. But the other half was like be the bigger man. So, I picked number two.

"I'll see what I can do."

"Troy! Come on, daddy!" She screamed from the bathroom.

"A'ight, I'll get back to you." I hung up and scurried off to Lexus. I pulled off the remainder of my clothes and got in the shower where she was. I pulled the glass door open, stepping in as the steam filled the area. She rubbed her hands down her wet body and pulled her into my chest.

"I'm sick of you talking shit. Bend over!" I demanded. She did what I said, and I put my semihard dick in her slowly. In response, she threw it back on me as she planted her hands firmly in the wall.

"Yeah, keep doing that shit Lexus. Get this shit back rock hard.

"Fuck, I love you baby." I slapped her ass and held onto her waist.

"I love you too Lex, now give me this good shit."

She knew how to take my mind off everything. But my mind was still wandering about Stephen and his little problem. Daddy's little son got his baggage, and it was some juicy shit at that.

Monet Dragun

Chapter Three
Troy

'When I pull up on a nigga, tell that nigga bag back,' I opened my eyes as I tried to adjust to the darkness. As my phone rang, Lex was laid up on me in a position that made me wanna have sex with her *again*. I was in love with her body. She ain't use to be this thick back in high school, but when she came of age, she grew into it. Don't get me wrong, I loved her curves back then, but I'm more in love with them now.

My phone started to ring again, so I extended my arm and grabbed it of the nightstand. My homeboy was calling me. It was too early for me to be leaving Lexus like this, but this was my job.

I answered it, with a tired strained voice. "Wuzzam'in, Marcus?" I questioned into the phone. While rubbing my eyes, I could hear the man cleaning and taking his glock apart. He was utterly ruthless.

"Sup, my nigga. I know it's early and shit and you probably laid up with Lex right now, but we gotta make some early drops and meet up with some rich folks that's tryna make a sale." I nodded as if he could see me. Lex moaned and shifted on me.

"Alright, is it the big deal they tryna sell? The rocks or the diamonds?" It was silent over on his line for a moment. And then I could hear the click of his glock.

"*Both*, my nigga." I was kind of shocked my damn self.

"Oh, *word?*" I said with surprise.

"Yup, they are giving up some hard bread for em' too." I stroked my chins hairs and Lex groaned again. I placed my hand on her bare ass, rubbing it just to sooth her baby self and continued to listen to Marcus.

"A'ight, I'ma be ready in a few. I'll meet you at the business." Lex looked up at me and pecked my lips. My girl was beautiful even when she woke up.

"Coo' bro. Deuces." The three beeps told me he had hung up. Looking at my phone to see I had a text message from Stephen. I shook my head and closed my phone then put it on the dresser.

Lex touched my face softly causing me to glance down to see Lex staring at me. "What?" I said kissing her forehead.

"You're leaving me?" She said sadly, the look on her face kind of broke my heart. "You know I'm coming back baby girl." She blinked batting her eyelashes.

"Troy? Sometimes, I get scared and think when you walk out that door, you'll never walk back through it again. Please, don't leave me, let you goons handle it." I haven't heard her talk like this in years.

"You know I'm not leaving you. Where is all this coming from?" I asked while knitted my eyes together in bemusement.

"Because you're getting big. I can't help but think or wonder and people are going to want what you have. I don't want you to get killed over this. I know I sound like I'm fourteen years old again, but I can't lose you, Troy. I just can't." I sighed and held her tight against me.

"Lex, you see all this we built? You see that rock on your finger? You see how we are now? You know what I see, though? I see that I won't be leaving this earth for you to be by yourself. When I die, it'll be when I'm old and gray. When we're both old and gray because I'm not leaving this earth without you, my love. I'll never leave you baby, you remember that. If there was something to happen, anything, you better believe I'm going to fight the shit." A little tear cascaded down her face.

"Troy, I love you so much. Please just hold me for a few minutes before you leave, please?" She asked.

"You know I will. You know I'm coming back. Don't doubt daddy, okay?" I said as I pulled her closer to me. I pulled her so close it was like we were one. She kissed on my neck and I rubbed on her ass. "Troy?"

"Hmm, mama?" I answered.

"Why is your dick so hard right now?" She giggled. I shook my head and kissed her forehead.

"Because you make it that way." I said softly. It was quiet for a moment.

"Troy?" She kisses my neck when she said it.

"Yes, Lexus?" She sighed.

"I'ma always be your rider. You remember that." Lexus swung her leg fully over my lower half and sat up on me as she looked down at all my tattoos. I was so mesmerized by her beauty man.

"I know you are mama. Damn, I love you. You got a nigga weak." I expressed as she giggled that giggle I loved so much. I sat up and kissed her stomach and held her so close to me. I pulled away while rubbing my hands up and down her back, kissing her flat stomach again, licking up to her bare chest. My lips went up to her neck and her held fell back.

"Baby." She whined. I couldn't help but want to make love to her. She twisted her hands in my hair as she brought her lips to mine. Making sure to stick her tongue in my mouth.

"You wanna ride daddy right quick before I leave?" I said against her weak soft flesh.

"Troy, just don't leave." Lex bit her lip then moaned out as I picked her up and slid her down on me. I didn't want her worrying so I put her mind to rest.

"You know I got to handle this business. Promise you, I'm not going nowhere from this earth." I moved her up and down on my dick as her words were replaced with moans. She closed her eyes alwhile she held onto me. "You trust me, Alexus?" I bounced her more on me and faster.

"Oh, yes! Baby I do!" She buried her face into my neck as I was hitting her spot in this position. "Then you know I'm coming back, right? You gone stop doubting me?"

Her moans got louder with each thrust. "Yes, Troy I know you're coming back! Fuck, baby don't do that!" She screamed, I smirked and knew exactly what she was talking about.

"What this?" I lifted her up high and slammed her down on me. She felt so right and wet.

"Yes! That shit!" I did it three more times hearing her scream my name turned me on, "Troy! Troy! God, Troyyyy! Fuck you, Troy! Uh!" I pulled her off and flipped her over hitting it form the side.

"Fuck me huh? Didn't I tell bout that!"

"Fuck, I'm sorry!" She screamed. We went at this for another hour. But I couldn't be late for this shit. I love my Lex so much, but the way she was talking made me realize I must be extra careful.

**

Fixing my hat, I hopped out of the car with Marcus on my trail. "Bro you good? It's like your mind been elsewhere." He was right. What Lex said weighed heavily on my heart.

"It's just somethings that Lexus told me. She been worrying about me and I ain't even know it. I thought we was past all that." He made the oh sound lowly.

"That talk is she alright?" Marcus probed.

"Yeah, I hope so, but let me get my mind right so we can get this deal." He nodded and we did our handshake. Ringing the doorbell, a big white man opened and stared down on us.

"Name?" He said strongly.

"Trojan Griffin." He nodded and stepped aside letting us in.

"Mr. Swiss is waiting on you in the den." We both nodded and walked towards the area. When we got down there, he sat there in all white looking at us. He had two pit bull dogs next to him with another bodyguard behind him.

"Hello, men. Have a seat." We sat at the other end of long marble table and looked at him with serious looks.

"So, I have the goods and I want artillery and drugs as part of the exchange."

"And the money?" He nodded, for the man behind him to give us the money. He poured the money on the table. It was stacks of hundred dollars bills. This was the biggest deal I ever made. I looked at Marcus, as he looked at me.

"We have a"

"Everyone put ya' hands up!" We all snapped are head at the perpetrator at the door dressed in all black. Damn! I can't believe this bullshit right now.

Chapter Four

"I said put your damn hands up fool!" I smirked. This shit had to be phony. It just had to be. Slacking my hands down, giving this punk the sorriest look ever.

"Nigga, you ain't fooling nobody! That's a damn toy gun in your hand." It was silent and Marcus looked over at me. He squinted his eyes and I nodded.

"This ain't no joke! Give me the damn drugs and money!" He said huskily through the mask. His voice almost sounded like the guard that was at the front door. I knew what was going on. I quickly grabbed the gun before he could blink twice. Twisting his wrist in the process, ready to break his shit.

"Now, who got the piece homeboy?" Marcus walked over to him and checked his pockets. I looked over at Mr. Swiss and he was applauding. "Good job. Now that that's over with and I know you're for real with are deal, Johnson, give him the goods. He's good people." He said with a grin. I nodded as Marcus took the mask off the guy's head. He was indeed the guard at the door. They couldn't play me even if they tried.

"So, this was a test?" Marcus questioned, obviously confused. He needed to stop smoking. For real.

"Yes, I wanted to truly know if you right for this great partnership." Mr. Swiss said in his deep British accent. "And a deal is a deal. Mr. Griffin? Nice doing business with you." He extended his hand and me and Marcus shook it. We were in the big leagues now. Next step is the city. Well maybe not the whole city. I'm just one black man.

Grabbing the bag off the long marble table, we made our way out of the establishment. The whole walk was silent. When we got into my car, his mouth exploded with a thousand words.

"Mane, what type of game was that? I ain't no punk, but damn. I thought that shit was real." He said to me, as his eyes was glued to his phone.

"I just had a feeling that it was fake. Now, I'd have a different feeling if it wasn't. We just gotta be careful out hea' homie. And, for real, do not tell Lex about this. She already cried her eyes out to me this morning. I damn sure don't want her almost having a heart attack and being real upset with me, a'ight?" He nodded and I pulled off from the big mansion. If it wasn't my girl to worry, who else was it to worry about me? My mama wasn't on this earth anymore, but I knew she was watching over me.

If I could get my mom back, I'd do anything, but that was all a dream. Switching my left hand with my right on the steering wheel as we cruised back to the club, my phone started to buzz.

"Aye, why is your brother calling you?" Marcus questioned as he looked down at my phone.

"Oh, yeah I forgot to tell you about that. Last night he called me saying he needed some help. And he wanted in." He took one good look at me and burst into laughter.

"Two left feet Stephen? Wants in? Into what? Hell, if that was possible! He'd trip in fall on his own. He ain't getting into shit, Troy. Don't trust that two faced ass nigga." He said wiping a little tear out of his eye. "But, with all seriousness. Why does he want into the game? Even though he ain't." I sighed.

"Because his dumb ass was taking steroids and they found out. Now he is kicked off the team for good, my mans." Turning on our street, my phone started to ring again. "I'ma just answer it. Ion' feel like being damn annoyed." I didn't feel like having the police on my ass either. Especially with this amount of cash and drugs on me. Plus, two black men in a nice car? Not a good mix for the Feds.

So, I answered the call on my iPhone watch. I didn't bother to see exactly who it was. I just answered it.

"Sup? Mane why you keep calling me." I said in an angered tone.

"Well, excuse the hell out of me for calling my man to see how he was doing?" I cursed myself for not looking at the caller ID. Looking over at Marcus, I shot him the middle finger. He covered his mouth, to hush his chuckles.

"Oh, oh hey baby! I'm sorry. My brother been calling my phone, about what I told you last night. Sorry for being rude." I said with a now softer tone. A nigga didn't want to be in the doghouse. I could her Marcus snickering and I darted my eyes at him again.

"Mhm, so Ciara called me crying and she wants to come over. Is that fine?"

"Sure, as long as he doesn't come over my crib. I don't need his freeloading ass at my house, with his corn chip smelling ass feet. Yeah, but please can it just be her and my little niece?" I pleaded. I could just hear her giggling.

"It's going to be them two anyway. She said she had something important to tell me. I don't know about what though." I shrugged my shoulders as I turned into my business parking lot.

"So?"

"Hey, little sis how you been! I miss you, fat momma!" Marcus called out and cut me off. How rude?

"I'm fine, love. You better not be getting my Troy in any trouble or that's your ass." He held his hand to his heart like she broke it up into tiny pieces.

"I would never!" I laughed and mushed him.

"This fool can get his own self into trouble without my help. But I gotta take care of business. I'll talk to you later pookie. Love you."

Her sweet voice bomb through the phone. "I love you too pumpkin, be careful Troy." Before I could say another word, she hung up. I shook my head as I laughed. Marcus looked at me and I put my hand up for him to hush.

"Don't say a word." I said to him with a straight face. He busted out laughing as he got out the car. I popped the trunk, and we got the bags. I heard my name be shouted from across the way. I looked up to see my damn brother.

"Hell, he doing hea'? How he…" I cut Marcus off.

"Take this in the biz, dawg. Them stack need to be counted. Lemme handle my bro." He dapped me up and nodded as he grabbed the black heavyduty duffle bags and walked into out twostory building. I closed the trunk and turned my attention to Stephen. "Sup? What you are doing here?" I questioned.

"I really need your help. I know we not on the best beat of terms right now. But I'm goin' through something. Bro, help me out." Never thought he'd be coming for a handout.

Chapter Five

"What do you want man? Why you here in the first place? How you even find out where I worked?" I questioned all in one breath.

He leaned back against his car and folded his arms. "Everyone knows the big Troy Griffin. It wasn't hard. But can we put our differences aside? I really need your dire help. I have a baby to support and a girl. It's my fault that I got kicked off them team. I was never you."

Yeah whatever, nigga you a bluff.

"Face it, Stephen. This life ain't for you. Go ask father for a handout or go work at the church." I shrugged and began to walk away from him.

I didn't want him in my business and there were two reasons for that. One, I didn't trust him. I didn't even trust him with my life, and he was my blood. Two, he wasn't worth my payroll.

"Bro, so you gone do ya' blood like that?" he called out to me, trying to muster a hurt expression on his face.

I waved him off as we stood there staring at one another. There was an awkward silence before he decided to speak up again.

"We blood man."

"Were we blood when you wanted to runtellthat to pops? Nah. Now, we blood because you need my help? Fuck outta here, Stephen. You can miss me with that bullshit." I spat, stroking my beard.

I was getting tired of his 'We blood' antics every time his ass needed my help. Blood would never mistreat you the way Stephen mistreated me.

He looked at me with sincere eyes before running his hand over the top of his head. "Troy man, I was jealous of you."

"Jealous of me? You're pops golden boy, not me." I chuckled in disbelief while simultaneously shaking my head.

"That's what it seems like to you and to everyone else, but lately, you were all he seemed to talk about. It was always 'Troy this' and 'Troy that.' I envied the fact that dad was starting to notice you more than me. So, I did what I had to do. You kinda helped me out when you gave that whole speech." He scratched the back of his neck nervously.

I looked at him, my mouth hanging slightly open at his words, "You're fuckin' pathetic."

I turned away from him, starting my walk into the building. My mind was racing a mile a minute. Not at the fact that Stephen wanted a part of my wealth, even though that was a shock, but at my father. The fact that he mentioned my name in a manner that made Stephen jealous of me came as a surprise.

"Man, Troy! Troy!" Stephen called after me, hot on my heels.

I spun around and smacked my teeth, "Nigga what?"

"You really gon' do this to me bro? I got a daughter to feed. Your niece needs this money too, it's not just for me." his head dropped low.

I sighed loudly, exclaiming my frustration. I stared up at the sky, contemplating my next choice of words.

As much as I despised Stephen and his ways, Ciara and my niece didn't deserve that. Afterall, Ciara was a pretty down chick, whom my brother didn't deserve, and my niece was just a baby. If it was just Stephen struggling, I could've easily told him to get a job at the nearest McDonald's and get the fuck out of my face, but it wasn't just him. He had a family. A family with my blood running through it, and they didn't deserve to suffer.

"Follow me." I mumbled, motioning him to come into the building.

"Yyou fa'real?" he replied, the shock evident in his voice.

"Yyes I'm fa'real nigga!" I mocked him, "Hurry up before I change my mind."

He trailed behind me as I walked past most of my crew and into the room where Marcus was. I cleared my throat, causing him to look up. Him and Stephen glanced at each other and I couldn't help but notice the uneasy look that came over his face.

He stood up and jammed his hands in his pocket, nodding his head towards Stephen, "What's golden boy doin' here?" Marcus probed as he scrunched up his nose.

"He apart of our crew now." I shrugged, "Ayo Mali, show him how to pack this up."

Mali, another one of the crew members nodded, beckoning for Stephen to come over to her. She bit her lip in approval of his stature.

"Uh uh, Mali, he's taken." She rolled her eyes at me with amusement. All the while, Stephen looked amazed at the things we were doing.

"Aye, you trust him?" Marcus asked, as he leaned next to me. He gave him a once over and started to talk again. "He looks too shady to me, dawg."

I looked over at Stephen who was cluelessly following Mali's directions, before shaking my head. "Nah. To be honest, you're more of a brother to me than he ever will be, bruh."

Marcus grinned before dapping me up. "That's how it always will be."

"We just gon' have to keep our eyes on him." I said sternly. "Your fam can be your worst enemies." I walked past them and made my way to my office. Marcus continued to eye him. It was something about the look he was giving him that made me think he hated Stephen on a whole different level that I did. But I just let it slide if it was something out of the norm. It was bound to come out.

***

Taking out my keys and approaching my front door, the chatters of two loud ladies filled my ears. Before I could even put the key in to unlock the door, it flew open. My beautiful girl stood there with her arms wide for me to walk into.

"Hey, my love." She said squeezing my in a tight embrace.

"Hey, what you two in here giffy gaffy'in about huh?" I questioned as I sat my keys down on the side table.

"Bro-in-law, it's something I need to tell you." Ciara said as she stood inches from the kitchen. She fiddled with her fingers as she looked at me. Her eyes were turning red, and she looked as if she was holding back tears.

"What's the matter? Y'all were just laughing and stuff. What changed?" I said with a look of concern on my face.

"Baby, we were. I have no clue why she's like this. Girl, you okay?" Lex said rubbing her back trying to confront her in some way.

"I um, the baby isn't Stephen's, and I don't know how to tell him. Please, Troy don't tell him. He really wanted this baby." She pleaded.

"I don't even like his ass…" Lex slapped me across the chest.

"Stop it, Troy! Jesus." Lex hissed. I shrugged and ran my hand over my rough blond and brown curls.

"No, Lex, he has every right to hate him. It's true. Stephen is nothing but a damn lair! Do you know how many women he slept with? All the lies and deceit he's caused? I'm even lucky to be pregnant with the many miscarriages he's caused me. I loved him and I still do. But I can't tell him this baby isn't his. He hasn't suspected anything, and I want to keep it that way." She said wiping her tears with a tissue that Lex had just handed her.

"Well, who is the father Ciara? You know I can hold water." I said bringing her into a nice hug. But she pulled away.

"If I tell you I know you're going to spill the beans. You won't be able to keep quiet about this one." I knitted my eyebrows together. What did she mean by that?

"You don't trust me? Or Lex?" She nodded.

"I do trust you two, but that's not it's just my lover is closer to you more than you know." Lex looked at me and I was left dumbfounded.

"Please, don't tell me what I think you'reb telling me?" She nodded and my mouth was left wide the hell open. I felt Lex's small fingers run under my chin and pushed my mouth closed. She gave me that look. The look of "you better not". I sighed and watched as she walked away to tend to Ciara, who was crushed. Now I was thinking of how this situation was about to go. I had a niece on the way from someone I truly called my blood brother, even if it was Stephen's baby, she was my niece regardless.

Today, I accepted my brother in and then comes this? What can possibly happen next? Lord, help me please.

Monet Dragun

Chapter Six

"Lex." I called out.

Her light snores filled my ears, as I laid there with my eyes glued to the ceiling. One hand tucked in my boxers and the other behind my head. I moved from side to side, trying to get her attention.

"Lexus." I called out again, this time a little louder.

She was still knocked out. Damn this girl was a deep sleeper. I pulled my hand out of my boxers and slapped her ass lightly.

"God, Troy what do you want? I was having a dream about Kofi Siriboe!" She groaned.

"A dream about who? Lex, don't get fucked up, ya' hear?"

She giggled and turned over to me, as she slightly rubbed her eyes, "What baby?"

"You think I did the right thing, you know, by letting Stephen in my business?" I questioned still looking up at the ceiling.

I could feel her prop herself on her elbows. "You did what now? When was this!" She said dramatically.

I deeply sighed before speaking. "Yesterday babe. This nigga needed some damn help. So, I gave him some. Was I wrong for doing so?"

"Hell yeah!" Lex said while sighing and paused before pecking my neck softly. "I think you were just doing something...something like your momma would."

I sighed once again. I felt her soft index finger trace my tattoo of her name with a queen crown on top of it.

"You think? As much I want to keep this positive. I don't think I can trust him, like truly. For all I know, he could be working with the Feds or doing drugs or trying to steal from me. I don't know what the hell to believe, Lexus. This shit was a mistake." I rambled.

She rubbed her hand down my face. "Stop doing that. Stop beating yourself up over this. You got eyes everywhere, right? Keep an eye on him, and please don't be petty and slip up and tell

40

him the baby ain't his. I know you like to hit way below the belt when your anger gets the best of you."

I inhaled and let out yet another deep breath.

"Can you please stop blowing your hot ass breath on me? Geez Troy, the hell did you eat before you went to bed?" she laughed, mugging me.

I cut my eyes at her. "You knew what I ate before I went to bed babe. Your stank pussy." I began before she covered my mouth with her hand.

"Watch your mouth now, before I get in that ass." she plucked my forehead with her free hand.

I chuckled and moved her hand, trying to be serious.

"But, for real, I can't believe the sweet Ciara I knew, cheated and got pregnant by another man. My homeboy."

My phone started to buzz, and I looked over at it. Marcus' name flashed across the screen. Lex shrugged and laid her head on my chest, almost going to sleep during the moment.

"Wazzam'in?" I said as I rubbed my tired eyes.

"Why did Ciara calling me crying? I haven't talked to that girl in a long ass time." Marcus replied, a tad bit of worry in his voice.

Sure, you haven't.

"She is going through something with her man, I guess." I shrugged, trying to bite my tongue.

I looked down to see Lexus knocked out, I slipped from under her and made my way out on the balcony. I didn't want to disturb her sleep.

"I'm not surprised. He's full of bullshit anyway." He said coldly into the phone.

"I mean you right, he's an asswipe. But, let me ask you something, and be real honest with me. Have you ever, you know messed around with Ciara?" I stroked my beard waiting for his response.

He cleared his throat, and I could hear some shuffling in the background. "You my brother, I wouldn't keep it nothing but a hunnit' with you. We messed around for a while. I sorta was like her boyfriend number two."

We both chuckled. "What happened between y'all?"

"We kicked it when I found her crying at the park over that piece of shit. It kinda just went off from there," he sighed heavily, "Then suddenly she called me one day and told me she didn't want anything to do with me because she loved your brother. She changed her number on me, and next thing I know, her and Stephen moved to a different city and boom she's pregnant with his kid. I was lowkey crushed."

"That's why you can't stand that nigga huh?" I shook my head with a light laugh.

He chuckled. "Yeah. He got something he doesn't deserve. A beautiful daughter and a bomb ass girlfriend, that should be mine."

I let out a heavy sigh and ran my hand down the side of my face, "You ever think that, you know, the"

"You're not trying to tell me what I think you're trying to tell me?" he asked, tension sitting in his voice.

"That's exactly what I'm trying to tell you, but bro you can't let her know I let the cat out the bag." I mumbled.

"But that's my baby bruh!" he snapped.

"I know, I know, but give her some time. If she don't tell you in a week or so, let me know. I'll handle it."

He huffed and there was a long pause over the phone. "I just miss her man. How she gon' let that bitch nigga father my daughter? How? She let him hurt her so many times. So many nights she cried to me over the phone. So many times, she wanted me to do what he couldn't. Man, I loved that girl." He stopped talking and I could tell he was hurting. "I know I sound like a female right na', but she is letting him claim what's mine."

Looking at the night sky, I let all his words soak in.

"How would you feel if Lexus did that bull?" He questioned.

"I'd be pissed too. I'd want to kill that nigga, but for real when you see him at the biz, don't do or say nothing. Just keep it coo' you feel me?" He huffed and cursed under his breath.

"A'ight, man I'll keep quiet for na'. I gotta get some sleep. One love." I nodded and looked back in the house to see Lex spread across the bed.

"A'ight, one love." the phone beeped telling me he had hung up.

I looked at the time on my phone. It was 4:30 a.m. and I haven't had no sleep whatsoever. Sighing I walked back into the house and looked down at Lex. She was deep sleeper who slept wild anyway. I rubbed my tired eyes once again and just grabbed my pillow and walked out of the room. I needed at least an hour of good sleep before I got up officially in the morning to get on my grind. I couldn't even go to sleep because all this talk about secrets, was keeping me on my toes.

I shook my head quickly, running a hand down my face. I just decided to lay down with my baby. Walking back into the room, I slid back into bed with Lex. She immediately shifted when she felt me and laid on my chest, as I stared at the ceiling, attempting to sleep.

"What's wrong papi? Why aren't you sleepin'?" she mumbled against my chest, which caused me to smile at the fact she knew me like the back of her hand.

"Just thinking." I shrugged.

"About?" she replied tiredly.

I shifted a little, running my fingers through her hair. "You wouldn't keep any secrets from me, would you?"

There was a pause of uncertainty that filled the room that made me regret my question. Finally, Lex spoke up.

"Of course not, and you know that. Stop overthinking things and get some rest my love, for me." she pecked my lips repeatedly, before dozing off again. I had an uneasy feeling. She never just rushed off or brushed our conversations under the rug like that. Something was up, and I was determined to find out what it was exactly.

"Alexus?" I could feel her heart rate picking up and her palms began to sweat. All the signs that I knew she was keeping something from me. "Alexus Tiffany Walker I know you hear me talking to you guh'. You keeping secrets from me? And don't lie to me!" She sighed and propped herself up on her elbows. She knew I was upset when I said her full name.

"Troy ba"

"Do not Troy baby me! What's going on seriously? What are you hiding stuff from your man for?" I said looking deep into her eyes. She knew I hated liars.

"I didn't know how to tell you, Troy. We're young. You're in the game, and how am I supposed to know you going to be okay? And well" She said, and I knew the tears were about to flow.

"Baby, we had this talk, didn't we? You know"

"I know nothing! Troy, I don't know what to expect from this," she paused and grabbed my hand and put it on her stomach. "This is why I'm scared, okay?" She threw my hand off her stomach and got up crying. I just laid there like an idiot. It wasn't a bad secret she was keeping. She just didn't know how to tell me she was pregnant. I knew because my baby was getting them hips Yo. That weight was showing. I deeply sighed and got up from the bed. I knew I wouldn't get any sleep tonight.

"Lexus? Baby come out I'm sorry." I practically begged. Nothing, but silence filled the entire room. "Lex, please? Just come out and talk to me. I didn't mean to yell at you, love muffin." I heard a few giggles and cries. And I smiled because she loved when I called her that.

The door slightly opened, and she appeared with those big hazel brown eyes that were beautiful, but they were filled with tears. "Baby, come here. I didn't mean to yell. I just got a lot going on at once. But that doesn't give me the right to snap off on you." I held her close as I pecked her forehead. She wrapped her tiny arms around my waist as I heard her sniffling.

"And you telling me you're pregnant? How far along are you? Do you know how happy I feel right now? To know you're going to have my first child? Baby, I ain't leaving this earth no time soon, and I want you to stop worrying for the baby's sake. Lexus, you mean the world to me and on my momma's grave, I'm not about to leave you and my child to fend fa' y'all self. I love you girl. I can't believe I'ma be a daddy man." I could tell she was smiling.

"I'm four months, I didn't want to stress you out. You know with you being in the streets, I didn't want you worrying about me too. I'm sorry I didn't tell you sooner. And Troy?" I stood there holding her close to me.

"Yeah, love?"

"Nothing. I love you." I smiled at her comment.

"I love you too, baby. I already knew. I'm not mad my love."

***

Walking into my business, I heard arguing and shouting. "The hell?" I looked around seeing Stephen in Marcus' face for some reason. I didn't understand till I got closer and could hear their conversation.

"Don't tell me how to treat my girl mane! Worry 'bout yo'self." He shouted. Marcus was fuming, and I knew that look on his face all too well. I knew at any moment he was going to explode. So, I stepped into the fire and put it out.

"Aye! The hell is all this shoutin' and shit. Get back to work ain't shit to see here! Now!" Everyone's whispers and chatters just made me rub my temples. "Why are you to arguing like some females?" Marcus didn't say a word, his fist connected with Stephen's jaw before I could even stop him.

Marcus grabbed him up and slammed him against the wall.

"Yo! You ever disrespect her again and Ima break every bone in your body, you feel me!" I pulled them apart and just gave Marcus a look. I couldn't have Ciara or my girl trying to kill me over this one.

So, I had to stop it. Even though I wanted to see Marcus beat his ass, I couldn't. "Aye you go take a breather now bro!" I pushed Stephen towards the door and I just glared at Marcus.

"Don't even say it! I need a drink." He snatched away from my grip and headed up the stairs. I just shook my head and looked at the mess they caused in my biz. "Someone come clean this shit up!" I looked around for Stephen, who was standing outside screaming at someone on the phone. Hopefully not Ciara, but by the looks of his face, it was something real off about him.

My phone started to buzz, and I walked towards the elevator to go to my humble office. Pressing the button, I pulled out my iPhone, I noticed it was my father who was calling.

"Fuck?" I said to myself as I looked down at the contact. "Thought I blocked his ass?" This had Stephen written all over it in my book.

I swear Stephen bet not have caused no drama.

Monet Dragun

Chapter Seven

I continued to look at the phone as my father called it back to back. Debating if I should or should not answer it, my door flew open and Marcus stood there breathing like a bull.

"Yo! Troy we gotta talk for real. My mind been reeling man. I can't stop thinking about Ciara and..." I cut him off and told him to sit down and take a breather.

"Man, we can't talk 'bout that here, a'ight? You gotta chill, yo' for real." I shook my head and grabbed at my beard.

He nodded and closed his eyes, counting to ten. I could just tell. He was red all in the face and I knew he was beyond angry. My phone started buzzing again and I groaned in irritation.

"Who that?" He said raising an eyebrow.

My fingers began to tap rapidly. Something I did when I was upset, agitated, annoyed, and irritated and of course, my father was causing all those emotions to hit me all at once.

"Troy?" Marcus' deep voice said, sounding almost calming.

"Man, it's my pops." I said rubbing my temples.

I couldn't take him calling my phone again. We hadn't talked in weeks. So, I just answered it, even though I didn't want too.

"Hello?" I said as I cleared my throat.

"Um. Hello Troy? Yyour father is in the hospital." I heard Melina voice croak into the phone. "Troy?"

"Yeah, yeah I hear you hold on please." I snapped, getting Marcus' attention, "Marcus, go get my brother now! It's important!"

He seen the look on my face and scurried out of my office.

"Ssorry Mel. What happened to him?" I questioned gathering some of my things.

"He had a major stroke. It's some things about your father that you need to know about." she sighed, and I could hear her sniffle.

"Things like what?" I slipped on my jacket and cut off the lights, rushing outside.

Stephen ran into me and fell. He stood up and dusted himself off before giving me a confused look. I shrugged and motioned for him to follow me into my car.

"He wants to ttell you himself, bbut after he's well, I'll be leaving him." she hiccupped with a hint of sadness in his voice.

I couldn't help but laugh light. I knew my dad would only stay faithful to Melina for so long. Him keeping his dick in his pants would only last for so long.

"A'ight, my brother and I are on our way." I hung up the phone and sighed heavily, starting up the car.

The ride was silent for the most part. My thoughts were keeping me on the tip of my toes about my dad. Did I give a fuck about him? Not really, but one of my parents is already dead and I wouldn't know how to feel if I lost my father.

"You gon' tell me what's goin' on?" Stephen snapped at me, as I rushed through traffic.

"I know you ain't yellin' at me like you lost yo' fuckin' mind." I spat, pulling into the hospital.

He huffed and got out, slamming my car door. I mugged him, and walked through the doors, approaching the lady at the front desk. Asking for where my father was, she was staring at Stephen like he was all that. Now I'm a believer of what Ciara was preaching.

"Curtis Griffin." I nodded at her, as she typed the name on the computer.

"Pops!?" Stephen interjected, "What happened to him?"

"Stroke." I waved him off, grabbing the slip from the lady and heading towards the elevator.

When we made it to the seventh floor, Melina was standing outside his room door, texting away on her phone. I gave her a weak hug, and a small smile before entering the room.

Stephen of course, ushered to my father's side, giving him a tight hug. The two began to have a conversation with each other like I wasn't even the room. Thankfully, Lex was calling me.

"Hey, baby." I answered quietly, stepping out of the room.

"Hey, where you at?" she asked. "I was about to cook dinner but didn't want to start if you won't be home until later."

"I'm at the hospital."

"The hospital?!" her frantic voice shrieked through the phone, "Troy, what happened?! Oh my God, I'm on my way!"

I chuckled lightly. "Alexus, I'm fine. It's my dad."

"Oh." She let out a loud sigh of relief. "Is he okay though?" She was smacking on something and the shit sounded good.

"He is now, but aye, I'll call you when I'm on my way home. He wants to talk to me." I told her, as Stephen motioned for me to come back in the room.

"Okay, I love you Troy." she reminded me, causing me to smile.

"I love you more." I replied, making kissy noises through the phone, which caused her to giggle.

I slipped my phone back into my pocket and walked inside the room. I stood across from my father and Stephen, waiting for him to say whatever he had to say.

He cleared his throat and started, "I had a bad stroke, and the doctors say it was because of stress."

His speech was slurred and slowed down, which meant the stroke had did some damage on him. I nodded my head, and he continued to go on.

"I was cheating on Melina with a few females and it caught up to me." he admitted at first.

I smirked and shook my head. "Ain't a surprise. Prolly, threw anotha' good woman down the drain." I mumbled.

He ignored my comment and continued, "I also have been taking out money."

I raised an eyebrow and seen him, and Stephen exchange a look. I shrugged it off and motioned my hands for him to continue.

"Money from the church to help ppay off some people I owe. I just needed to get the sharks off my back." he put emphasis on the word I.

"The church? Out of all places, the church?" I laughed and shook my head. "Those people trust you with their money, and you use it for your debt?"

"The gguys, they…"

"Whatever man, that's what you called me over here for? To tell me you are hurting more people?" I cut him off, obviously agitated.

"I'm ssorry Troy. I didn't mean tto hurt anyone. I didn't mean tto hhurt you. You're my sson, aand I love you." he breathed out heavily. "I need yyour help putting mmoney back."

I laughed dramatically and threw my hands up in the air. "Of course. You know, for a second, I was believing that you were sorry and loved me, but you prove me wrong again. You only love me because you need my money. Miss me wit' the bullshit. Stephen, you could stay here and play happy family, but I'm out. Maybe, you can give him the money. But OOP forgot you just got a job. Betta' save up homie."

I made sure to add my touch of hostility by flipping them both off and exiting out the room.

***

Stephen

Once Troy left the room, my father cut his eyes at me. I dropped his hands, and put my face in mine own hands, sighing heavily. This was truly all my fault.

"I can't kkeep doing this, it's killing me." my father spoke up, as I got up and stood over by the window.

"You don't think it's hurting me? Your old ass had to do was pay them off! But no you had to go piping hoes down! How long am I supposed to fake with him!" I snapped.

"I'm taking that money out for you, Stephen! You owe those guys that money! They keep harassing me." he cried. "Me! Not you, Lord knows I'm tryin'!"

"I'm working on that, Pops." I sighed, thinking back to my conversation with Rudy.

It was a simple plan. Get in with Troy, help Rudy take over his business, and I would be in the clear. He probably would be able to get me back my spot on the football team.

"I ggotta tell him StStephen. He's my son, and I ddo love him. I can't keep doing this to him. You're the troubled one not him!"

I looked at him like he had seven heads and went off. "You sure you wanna do that? Let's not forget I know that the sweet lil' lady he thinks is his mother, isn't!"

He looked at me shocked, "Yyou wouldn't."

"I would. I'd tell him all about how you cheated on MY mom, with a random lady and created him. Then I came along. I'd tell him all about how you made MY mom take care of him, and that the reason you hate him so much is because he loved her more than he ever loved you, and she isn't even related to him." I laughed, shaking my head, grabbing my coat.

"Sstephen."

"Don't try me." I mumbled, before escaping out the room. "You don't want all your dirt spilled out." I smirked as the door shut completely.

***

Troy

By the time I got home, it was late. I went into the kitchen and found the plate of food Lex had made for me in the microwave. After eating it, I took a quick shower and slipped into bed next to a sleeping Lex.

Her small frame melted into mine, as I held her close. I scooted down to her stomach and put my face against it, before rubbing it with my large hands.

"Hey lil' baby." I whispered. "I just wanted you to know, that I love you so much. I'm gon' remind you every day when you get here. I'm gon' hug you, and kiss you, and give you the whole wide world baby. I promise. I won't ever tell you I'm disappointed in you, or make you feel like crap. I'm gon' support you no matter what ya' dreams are."

I could feel a few tears slip out of my eyes as I spoke. "I swea' you and yo momma are the best things that ever happened to me." I heard Lex sigh and sniff as she rolled over looking at me.

"That was so deep babe. Don't cry. This is why I love you." She pecked my lips countless times and put her forehead against mine.

"I just want the best for him. I want what my father didn't give me Lex." she put her finger to my lips to hush me.

"Shh, Troy. I know. I know, but baby you must let that burden go. Just let it all go. You can't keep hurting yourself like this, you understand me?" I nodded and kissed her nose.

"You're the best Alexus. You truly are. I'm so glad I have someone like you, and bae?"

"Hmm?" She said ever so sweetly.

"I don't want to kill the moment, but you smell like pickles how many you eat girl?" She broke out laughing and kissed me.

"Uh, the whole jar. They were good. I was craving them and no, Troy you're the best. I'm so glad you my man, and our baby is going to love you to death." I rolled over on top of her and kissed her neck and lips.

"You make me so happy girl. You make all my problems go away. I'm so in love with you." She smiled and kissed me back.

"I'm in love with you Troy, now get you some rest. You need it. You had a stressful day." I nodded and got off her as I laid on my back. She snuggled against me as I stared up at the ceiling. Her little hands brushed across my face forcing me to close my eyes. "Go to sleep, Troy, my baby boy." I nodded and tried to drift off to sleep. But my mind was reeling.

"Should I give him the money?"

Chapter Eight

"Baby grind on me. Relax your mind take your time on me. Let me get deeper shawty ride on me. Now come and sex me till yo body gets weak. With slow grindin baby!" Lex sang as the bright ass sun beamed in my eyes.

I lifted squinting. Her voice got louder. I looked over at the time and my whole face dropped.

"Fuckin' 7 a.m. you gotta' be kidding me yo'!" I flung the cover off my and noticed Trojan Jr. was on morning wood right about now.

I fell back on the bed and groaned dramatically. "A nigga can't catch a break." I mumbled to myself.

I shot up out the bed and trucked over to the bathroom where Lexus was occupying it. Opening the door, the lyrics of Pretty Ricky blasted throughout the bathroom walls. I leaned against the doorframe and watched as her curvaceous body danced in the shower. I bit my lip as she rolled her hips and more. My baby was blessed. Indeed, she was. I had to speak up causing this was really turning me on.

"Having fun in there, baby girl?" She jumped at the sound of my deep and tantalizing voice.

"God, Troy! You scared the living daylights out of me! How long have you been in here staring at me like a creepo?" she asked as she slid the shower glass door open.

"Oh, for a good five minutes now. Your oh so sweet voice woke me up, love." I said with a hint of sarcasm.

"Oh, hush up." She said sassily with a giggle. "But? Um, can you get in with me before you go to work. I just been having a feeling in the pit of my stomach, babe. I just need you to hold me before you go. Okay?" I nodded and pulled down my boxers.

Her eyes widened and she ducked back into the shower.

"Why you always do that, Lex? You den' seen me bootyass naked more than a hundred times. And you seen my manhood, I don't know, everyday basically. Baby, this ain't nowhere near new to you." I said with a light chuckle.

"It's just that you gotten' bigger Troy. I can't help that you a gift from God." She said with a light smile. "And baby, your phone is lighting up over there."

I nodded and did a 360 exiting the bathroom and into our suprememaster bedroom.

Her sweet voice shouted after me with the words, "You have a nice tight booty too, baby! Make me wanna give it a squeeze!" I shook my head at her silliness and picked up my phone.

"The emergency, Trojan war distress call?!" I picked up the phone and answered it. "Wuzzam'in? This ya' boy Troy."

"Hello, mister Troy. We'd like to inform you that you have a mole in your bi'ness, and we are no longer in need of your services. We feel that our money isn't safe anymore in this partnership." Mr. Swiss' voice filled the receiver, and I couldn't believe what I was hearing.

"There isn't a mole in my biz! You my best seller. You can't back out on me now." I said rubbing my temples.

"Well, Rudy," he cleared his throat. "Has told me other wise, and I have to believe my own loyal employer. So therefore Mr. Griffin, our deal is off," The phone line went dead, and I was left shocked.

"Hello? HELLO!?" I stared at the phone, as I heard Lex shouting for me to come to her.

I was way beyond pissed. Why on earth do I have bad luck? Why is God sending me this turmoil? What did I do oh so wrong for this to be happening to me?

"Baby? You coming?" I heard Lex say to me as she still had the water running.

"Uh, yeah, bae!" I sent Marcus a quick text telling him what had just went down.

Shaking my head with the slightest anger, I walked towards the bathroom where she was still singing. Alexus' presence always made me feel good inside, even though this wasn't fixable. I slid the door open and stepped inside. Lex turned around with the brightest smile on her face, but when she seen my face, hers faded.

"Troy? Are you okay love?" She put her soft wet hand on my cheek and looked me deep into my eyes.

"It's nothing babe, really." I turned her around because her gaze was killing me.

She could get anything out of me with that look. I pulled her into me and held her close as I rubbed my rounding stomach. She was growing every day, and my baby was too.

"Troy?" I closed my eyes I knew this was coming.

"Yeah?" I answered lightly.

"How do you think our baby is going to look? Like me or you?" She said softly, as she kissed my hand.

"More so like you. I have too much of my dad in me. I want our baby to look like you, be smart like you, and have your personality. I'd rather him or her have my athletics. But I'd be damned if he or she get into what I'm into. I want our baby to have their own life. I want our baby to have their mind right and not have to go behind their parent's backs. I want him or her to understand that I love them unconditionally, and I don't regret having them." I could hear her sniffling. Her hormones were starting to get the best of her.

"Why you crying, mama?" I questioned with a small chuckle.

She shrugged and turned around and kissed my chin. "Because you're the best man I ever met. You're going to be the perfect father. You're nothing like your father. I want my son or daughter to look just like you. Act like you, be smart like the both of us and..."

I crashed my lips into hers. I loved her oh so much. She was the one to keep my head up, and right now she was going just that.

"I. Love. You. So. Much!" I said inbetween kisses.

I ran my hand through her thick black hair as she wrapped her small arms around my waist. In the matter of seconds, my manhood was growing and soon after her moans were filling my ears.

"I wish we could stay like this, but you have to go to work." She said in a overdramatize baby voice.

I picked her up and kept kissing on her. "I own that shit I can be late."

***

Stephen

I'm so tired of doing paperwork, paperwork, and more goddamn paperwork. When can I push the drugs and make some calls? I'm trying to get this nigga out of here.

"Here you go." I looked up to one of the assistances smiling down on me and holding out something for me to grab.

I looked her up and down and seen a lot I could grab. I knew exactly what to do at this point.

"Thank you uh"

"Mia. My name is Mia." She said with a smile as she pushed her hair back.

"Well, Mia how you doing today hunny? You are looking pretty good today." I said with a smirk. She immediately giggled and blushed as she pulled her hair back behind her ear.

"I'm doing fine, and what about you?" She said leaning down in front of me.

Her titties almost spilling out of her chest. I licked my lips and leaned closer to her and whispered in her ear.

"I'ma be doing you if you let me." I smirked.

She giggled again and nodded, writing something down. She slid me a piece of paper with her number on it.

"Call me." She placed the papers on my desk and walked away, making her ass bounce with each step.

I'll be using her to get what I need. I looked up again and seen Marcus looking at me sideways. I scoffed and shook my head and mumbled the words "fuck you". He nodded and walked over to me I stood up and before he could do anything Troy stepped in front of him to stop him.

"He ain't worth it dawg, let it go."

Marcus nodded, and cracked his knuckles as he walked away.

"Ain't yo' ass supposed to be working. Why you playing and shit?" Troy groaned. I was sick of his mouth already.

"I am working, the fuck." I shot back.

"Just fa' that, yo' ass will be unloading the trucks. Get to that shit." He threw a pair of gloves at me and I just mumbled something under my breath.

I'ma only take so much of this bull from him. I couldn't wait until my time was up, and Rudy gave me the time to shine.

***

I got home and stretched, listening to some of my bones crack. I didn't hear my baby girl blabbering, so I figured she must've been asleep. I took a deep breath in and didn't smell any food, which was weird because Ciara always was cooking by this time.

"Ciara!" I called out, only to be replied with silence. "CiCi!" I called her by her nickname.

I knew she only ignored me when she found out I cheated on her. I searched through my memory, trying to figure out what female I had been with last. It was either Trina or Rita. They were both two spiteful hoes who were mad I didn't want to be with them.

I jogged upstairs and pushed open our room door. "Ciara you'ont hear me calling..."

I stopped talking once I realized the empty room. I opened the closest to see all her clothes gone. I went over to my daughter's room and saw that all her stuff was gone too.

"What the fuck?" I mumbled to myself, scratching my neck as I went inside the kitchen.

There was a small piece of paper that was on the kitchen counter. I picked it up and sighed, reading the words.

'I'm done.'

***

Marcus

58

There were a few knocks at my door as I rolled out of bed. It was damn near twelve in the morning, and I was just falling asleep. I tucked my gun in my waist, just to be safe and stretched. I had a feeling it was Troy though, because all day long he been talking about a nigga named Rudy who messed up our deal with Mr. Swiss

"What the fuck bruh." I groaned, as a series of knocks hit my door again.

I opened the door to see Ciara and my daughter in her car seat. I quickly grabbed the car seat and pushed her inside because it was cold as fuck.

"I'm sorry it's late. I had nowhere to go."

"What about Stephen?" I spat, taking the cover off the car seat.

"I lleft him." she sniffed.

I nodded, trying my best to not let a smile form on my face. I looked down at the small baby in the car seat, who was now wide awake. She looked just like Ciara but had my eyes. My baby was truly beautiful.

"Hey daddy's baby." I smiled picking her up. "It's me. Yo' real daddy. I'm sorry I wasn't around for a little while, but I'm gon' make it up to you. Promise." I pecked her forehead.

"I'm sorry." Ciara wiped away a few of her tears.

I nodded, "What's her name?"

"Sophia." she smiled small.

"Sophia." I pecked my baby girl's forehead once more, before laying her on my chest.

"Can I?" Ciara asked, pulling out her phone to take a picture.

"Get my good side." I chuckled.

I watched her take a few pictures before she sat down. I pulled her body close to mine and pecked her lips.

"I love you Ci." I pecked her lips once more. "You don't ever have to worry about that nigga again."

She looked up at me and smiled. "I love you more Mar." I looked into her eyes. They were puffy like she had been crying for a while.

"Ciara?" She looked at me, and her bottom lip began to quiver she knew this was coming. "Don't do that crying, please?" She nodded and wiped her small tears. "Why you cut me off like that? Huh? I know you loved him, and I wanted to get you from under him." She sighed and laid her head on my shoulder. As she twirled her finger on my tattoos.

"Because..." She paused before she sniffled.

"Because what, Ciara? You can tell me." I stated as I ran my fingers through her short black hair.

"He would've hurt me. He would have hurt me bad if he found out, Mar. His temper has no mercy, and he would've beat me for cheating on him. Even though he cheated on me countless times and I stayed with him. But I couldn't take the hurt anymore and I couldn't keep her from you. I know how you are." I nodded and kissed the top of her head.

"He will not hurt you and that's a problem. I'll kill that nigga of he even come near you. And Ciara?"

"Yes, Marcus?" She said lowly.

"Thanks for giving her my grandma's maiden name. That means so much to me, girl." She looked up at me and kissed me.

"It's because you mean the world to me and she needs her real dad. A real man. I need you. Can you make love to me tonight, Marcus?" I pecked her lips not once but twice.

"I wouldn't have it any other way baby girl."

My phone buzzed and I looked at it as Ciara got off my lap and picked up my baby Sophia. "Take her to the guest room. I'll get y'all things later." She nodded and switched off.

"Was that Ciara voice I heard?!" I didn't even know he picked up that fast.

"Yeah, Troy. She left him man and I'm not letting her get away this time or my baby girl." I rubbed my hand down my face. "She's so beautiful."

"I know man, but we got a problem and it with our rival, Rudy." I sat up alert and wide awake now.

"That nigga back! Yo' we got figure this out. What Mr. Sw" he cut me off.

"He backed out man. I'm already stressed. I'll talk to you about this at the biz tomorrow. One love." He sounded overly stressed.

"Yeah, bro one love." The phone beeped three times and I just sat back and looked at the ceiling what we worked so hard for is not about to go down the drain. Promise ya' that.

"Baby?" Her voice was so soft.

"Here I," I shot up when I saw her naked body. "Oh, shit na' here I come!" I missed her ass so much it hurt.

Chapter Nine
Marcus

"Oh, my God Marcus!" She clawed at my back and moaned my name so loud.

Her voice made me wanna do more to her.

"Damn, girl shh you gone wake up the baby." She didn't have a care in the world. Her eyes were in the back of her head as I was hitting all her pleasure spots.

"I can't!" She whined as she wrapped her legs around around my waist, grabbing my butt for me to go deeper.

"Shit, girl! Have you had it in a while? You tryna kill me!" I groaned as she squeezed herself around my member.

"Hell no! I haven't had any since me and you had sex! Ffuck, Mmarcus! Aand that was nine months ago! St" I cut her off before she could even say anything. I didn't even want to hear her calling his name.

"You don't have to say it, Ciara." I flipped her over and she was now on top of me and sliding down on me.

Running her hands through her short hair, messing it up even more, I was driving her body insane.

"God, Marcus!"

"Just ride me baby." I groaned as I gripped her hips.

I was going to change her life, and she was going to change mine.

***

Laying on my stomach, I heard little babbling. I felt a tiny body on tip of my back. I smiled slightly and knew it was my little princess. Looking to the left and right of me, I didn't see or feel anyone in the bed with me.

"CiCi?" I spoke with a hint of worry in my voice, afraid that she had left.

"Yes?" She answered softly.

I seen the flash of the phone and heard the clicking noise. I let out a little chuckle as well as a sigh of relief. She was only taking a picture of me and my little princess.

"What time is it?" I yawned.

I felt her lift Sophia off me so I could roll over and stretch. "Uh, around onethirty in the afternoon."

I shot up and was about to jump out the bed before she stopped me with a laugh. "Relax, Troy called, and I told him you were sleep. He understood and said for you to come in later tonight. Something about "buisness to take care of." And y'all have to handle some people."

She shrugged and I nodded knowing exactly what he meant. I laid back down, as I slid my hands down my face.

"What you babbling about, Phia?" She said as she raised her in the air and nuzzled her nose making her giggle and drool.

"She wants her daddy, gimme." I smiled wide, reaching out for her.

Ciara playfully rolled her eyes and stood up from the bed, passing her to me. She was about to walk towards the bathroom, but her phone began to ring.

"So, he been blowing your phone up all morning huh?" I said with a little bit of anger.

"All night too." She sighed and walked to the bathroom, after she declined his call.

I was debating if I wanted to answer the next call she'd be getting, so instead I called Troy. Sophia tugged on my beard as she stared in my face, studying my every facial features. I was so busy admiring I didn't even notice that Troy had answered the phone.

"Sup, bro?" He spoke into the phone.

"Nothing, man I need some advice. It's about Ciara and this Stephen thing. I want to say something so bad, and rock his ass." I stressed.

"A time will come for that bruh. Just worry about Ciara and yo' kid, and how you gon' make up for whatever time you missed." he paused and cleared his throat, "But, you know he going to have to know that's not his baby someday."

I stroked my chins hairs as I thought on what he said. "You right. I'll at least give him that, but I swear to God, if he even comes near Ciara or my baby, I'ma kill him."

Sophia's lip began to quiver, and I knew the tears were about to come. "I'm sorry Phia, don't cry. I take it back. I'll let him live."

She smiled and showed her gums. She was just like her mama. "Damn, she just like Ciara. Don't believe them tears." Troy read my mind before we both broke out laughing.

"I got an idea. Somethin' real simple. Why don't I just send him the DNA test CiCi got done, with a picture of my and my little princess." I suggested, as Sophia played with my bottom lip.

He sighed and there was a long pause. "Fine, bruh. I don't like him anyway, and that idea ain't as petty as the shit I had in mind. Do what you please. Just don't let it escalate and his ass go crazy or some shit. You know I'd love to beat his ass with you, but Lex wants me to be civil."

I busted out laughing as he smacked his teeth. I looked down at Phia, who stopped playing with my bottom lip and had her thumb in her mouth and was in the verge of falling asleep.

"Aye, bruh?" I said smiling even though he couldn't see it.

"Wuzzam'in?" He probed.

"I think I done fell in love all over again. Baby girl is so precious mane." I rubbed her back gently.

"Ima be the same way bro. I know I am." he spoke excitedly. "But aye! Get ya' ass down here soon. We got shit to handle."

I nodded as if he could see me, "Ima be in there soon. I just want to spend time with my baby."

We hung up after saying our goodbyes. I looked down at her and she was fully asleep now. Her little snores were so cute. I took out my phone and took a picture of us. My phone vibrated with a text message from Troy.

"Damn, my boy knows how to come through and waste no time." I laughed.

He sent me Stephen's phone number, and I was about to play dirty just like him. I sent the picture of me and Sophia to his phone with the text. "Ain't life good. For me at least. You lost yo' job, girl, and baby. I picked it up for ya though. Oh, and note, peep out the DNA test in the background you might wanna zoom in Nigga☐"

I laughed at my antics, and pecked Sophia, "Daddy got'chu no matter what baby."

***
Troy

"Baby." Lex spoke softly into the phone.

"What is it baby?" I replied, looking through papers on my desk.

"Nothing, I just wanted to hear your voice." she giggled, "What'cha doin'?"

"Same thing I was doin' five minutes ago, Lex." I laughed.

She called me earlier and told me she just wanted to stay on the phone with me. I left her on speaker the whole time I was sorting things out. It really didn't bother me. In all honesty, her voice put me at ease and stopped me from going insane.

"Oh, yeah. Sorry." she giggled again, "We miss you, Troy."

"We?" I furrowed my eyebrows, before realizing she was talking about my baby, "Oh, nevermind. I miss my babies more."

"Wanna know what we did today?" she said, smacking on her food.

"Enlighten me, princess."

"Well, okay. We woke up and had breakfast. It was a nice combination of ice cream and waffles. Then, we took a nice walk around town and…"

"What the fuck this bitch ass nigga mean I'm out of a job?!" Stephen barged in my office, his face red.

I looked up at him and shook my head with a smirk, "Baby I'ma call you right back."

"Troy Griffin, I swear if you hang up this…" I hung up the phone, knowing I was going to hear her mouth later.

"Why he wit' my baby, Troy?" he said through gritted teeth.

"His baby." I corrected. "You're no longer needed here."

"What?" he scrunched up his nose.

"You heard me. You're dismissed Stephen." I shooed him away, looking back at my papers.

"I need this job to take care of me and mine though Troy. You ain't gon' help me out?" he smacked his teeth.

"What's yours? Ciara sho' ain't, and that lil' cute baby damn straight don't belong to you either. If I recall, I gave you this job to take care of Sophia. Seeing as she ain't yours, and my brother got her taken care of, I don't have any reason to pity your sorry ass. You don't make or break my business anyway, buddy. Now, can you please show yourself out?" I spat, before looking up at him with a smile.

"Oh, so he your brother now?" he laughed. "Damn, first you don't get to meet your real momma, and now you don't even know your real brother."

I shot up from my seat, and grabbed him by his neck, pinning him against the wall, "Fuck you say about my momma?!"

"She. Ain't. Yo'. Momma." he said through deep breaths with a smile.

I remember Lex told me keep it civil, but at that point, I couldn't. I began to beat his face in with my fist, all while choking him. He tried kicking me, but I dropped him and let him scurry around the floor. He finally got up, and swung at me, getting me in my upper lip.

I punched him square in his nose, and watched as he stumbled back, falling over a chair. I stomped on his body repeatedly, listening to him cough up blood.

"Troy! Troy bruh! You gotta stop. You gon' kill him!" I heard Marcus yell, as he pulled me away. "Even though, I wouldn't mind." he mumbled lowly.

"Fuck that nigga! Don't ever talk about my momma again bitch!" I yelled, running back over to him, and stomping on his chest.

Marcus pulled me away again and pushed me towards the other side of the room, "Calm the fuck down. What happened to all that he ain't worth it shit?"

"Fuck that!" I growled, growing even angrier.

Stephen stumbled to get up and leaned against the wall catching his breath with a bloody smile. Marcus and I both looked at him like he had six heads. Just seeing this nigga have that dirty ass smile made me want to kill him.

"Y'all gon' get y'alls one day." he laughed, limping away, "Rudy got y'all."

"Rudy?!" Marcus and I both called out.

Marcus snatched Stephen up by the back of his shirt and grabbed his phone. He hit Stephen in the back of his head, knocking him out. I watched as Marcus typed something into the phone and slipped it into his back pocket.

"We got a meetin' wit' Rudy in an hour at tha' spot. Get yo' guns ready, he only expectin' yo brother." Marcus informed.

I nodded and took a few deep breaths in. "Aye, Mr. Swiss said he was informed by Rudy that a mole was in the biz'."

"And this piece of shit knew, Rudy?" Marcus chuckled, shaking his head. "He was the mole."

"So, could it be possible Rudy tryna set up Mr. Swiss?" I assumed, spitting out some blood from when Stephen punched me.

"Aye, I ain't think of that." Marcus stroked his beard. "We could use that to our advantage and get Mr. Swiss back on our good side."

I nodded and walked back over to my desk, picking up my phone. A text from Lex was there. *I told you not to hang up, and what do you do? You hang up. I don't even know if you're good right now, Troy. Don't expect me to be here when you come home, I'll be at my moms.*

"Fuck!" I shouted, throwing my head back in frustration.

"What?" Marcus looked at me weirdly.

"Alexus bruh." I showed him the text. "We was on the phone when this lil bitch marched in here."

He shook his head, "I'll call her, or have Ciara talk to her. Don't even stress it right now bruh. Like I said, we meet Rudy in one hour."

***

I straightened out my chain and sat patiently in the car, waiting for this Rudy character and his people to walk into the building before us.

Alexus was on my mind heavy. I knew I should've never hung up, and she probably worried herself sick. I sent her text message, after text message, and got nothing in reply. Marcus called her, but she didn't answer. He said my best bet was to just let her cool off, so I decided to do exactly that.

"Let's go bruh." Marcus tapped my shoulder, pointing to three men walking inside the building.

I nodded and stuffed my gun into my waistband, stepping out of the car. As Marcus, a few other workers, and I made it inside the building, Stephen's menacing smile still was flashed inside my mind. It was disgusting how he could set up his own flesh and blood, but as I said many times before, he was no brother of mine. I had that feeling in my soul.

"You ain't Stephen." A man furrowed his eyebrows as we approached him.

"Sure ain't, but I'm guessin' you're Rudy?" I laughed.

He smirked, "That's my name."

"Then you're exactly the man I'm looking fa'." He nodded and motioned for us to have a seat. I readjusted my gun. Ready to pull it out at any moment.

"So, what can I do fo' ya?" He said with this looking upon his face.

"I'ma be straight forward. What biz was up on with my br'" I cleared my throat. I didn't want to call him my brother. "I mean, Stephen." His name made me cringe.

"And who are you to him? That ain't none of ya damn bi'ness." He said with a scrunchedup face.

"Oh, it has everything to do with us." Me and Marcus looked at each other and made a silent prayer that we'd both make it home to our babies tonight.

Chapter Ten

Marcus

"Oh, it has everything to do with us." I looked at Troy and he looked at me.

Rudy had the glummest look on his face. "What has everything to do with y'all? Ain't shit to do with y'all!" He said getting louder.

"Get the bass out your speech homeboy. So what's up with you and Mr. Swiss huh? Plotting on him too?" Troy said boldly.

"Man, fuck you talm' 'bout yo'? That's my boss. Ima loyal..." I cut him off and eyed him.

"You ain't loyal for shit. You tryna take him for all he got!" He began to chuckle lightly.

"What I do to get my paper and my drugs don't got shit to do with you. The shit I do with the old white trash is none of your bi'ness. I'll take him for all his riches and yours too! You just don't know who you're fucking with, huh?" Me and Troy both laughed. I made sure to have my phones recording app rolling because, this nigga was done for. Our boys were in ther right position, just in case he pulled something.

"So ya' brother, did you know he was taking you for all you had? Mane, I got half of yo' shit in the bank and nigga you won't make it out of here to see it." He smirked.

"You sure about that? We got yo' whole confession recorded and we had Mr. Swiss on the line the entire time we been here. So, who's the loyal one nah? Cat got your tongue?" Troy said as he sat back.

"And all the money you said you so called stole from us? Oh, we got that shit. You just to blind to know who works for you as well homie." I chuckled. He was fuming. His face was filled with anger. You could just see it.

"So, would you like to talk to ya' boss? Huh, go ahead?" Troy taunted. I could see his jaw tensing up. His hand moved for something under the desk and I knew exactly what he was going for. I nodded for Bucum to stay alert. He got the message and stepped closer to me and Troy, as he kept a firm grip on his gun.

"So, how's you baby momma? What's her name? Oh, Alexus? And, your dad Curtis? Oh, how about your mother"

"Don't speak about my girl or my mother!" Troy shot up, slamming his fist down on the table. His jaw was twitching, and his fingers kept thumping against the table. His was going to blow.

Rudy laughed and kicked his feet up. "My dad got in 'dat befo'. To think we may have been brothers. Oh wait, she ain't yo momma. Melina is." He said as he threw his head back in laughter. Before he could even look up, Troy shot up from his seat and pulled his gun out from the back of his pants.

Three shots rang off, and Rudy's body fell. His 'men' just stood there and nodded their heads at us.

"So y'all ain't gon' do shit?" I questioned, holding my gun out sideways.

"We work fa' Mr. Swiss." He shrugged.

"Glad yo' boy took this rat out. I was gettin' tired of his muh'fuckin' mouth. Mr. Swiss put some shit in'a back of a car out front fa' ya workers to flip." The big bald guy said to us with a nod.

I picked up the phone where Mr. Swiss was still on the line. "These niggas tellin' the truth, or we gotta kill 'em?" I said as I raised an eyebrow as I looked down at Troy. His face was twisted, and he was shaking.

"They tha' real deal, Mr. Marcus. I appreciate ya findin' tha' real problem. Tell Troy God bless, and Rudy always talks out his ass. Don't pay any attention to his ass." He told me in his British accent. He didn't know his "loyal worker" was dead, as I looked up at Troy.

He walked out of the building with tears streaming down his face. Was he crying because he killed a man? I highly doubt it. Was he crying because someone brought up his mother in yet another hostile manner? That most likely was the cause.

"Thank ya' Mr. Swiss. It's been nice doin' business with you." I thanked him before we both hung up.

I followed Troy out to the car where he was already inside, leaning his head against the window. I looked him over and saw him fidgeting with his fingers.

"I'on want you at home by yo'self bruh. You gon' spend the night at my crib, a'ight? I'll give Alexus a call on mo' time." I told him, as he silently nodded.

I couldn't believe I was seeing my bestfriend break down like that. It was sad to even hear it or see it.

***

Alexus

"Let's say I read you a book, peanut. I'm guessin' you'd like that." I mumbled, running my hands over my small pudge.

Grabbing the BookFiend the shelf, wondering if I was having a sweet little girl or a rowdy boy like his father. I smiled at the thought as I opened the book and laid out on the bed in my old room of my mother's house. As soon as I got comfortable, I heard a soft knock on my door, and I knew it was her.

"Come in, mommy!" I called out, not wanting to leave the bed.

She walked in with a small smile and my cellphone. "Someone named Marcus is calling you again."

"Just let it ring." I whispered softly. "Has he called again?"

She looked down on my phone and scrolled, before shaking her head. "He just sent a text that said he loves you and he's sorry. Is this Troy texting from another mans phone?" She probed. I nodded and sighed as I put down the baby book.

"I'm not overreacting, am I?" I asked her, as she sat at the edge of my bed.

I saw her smile a little. "Just a bit baby. I mean he was hanging up, so you didn't have to hear the nonsense. He didn't want to stress you. You know his line of work." She stated as she rubbed my leg.

"But mom not knowing what could have happened next stressed the fuck out of me! I already knew it was his piece of shit brother!" I groaned, letting my anger get the best of me.

"I understand, but he's just trying to protect you Lex," she reasoned with me. "I say you hear him out, okay?"

I nodded and grabbed my phone from the dresser. I called Marcus back, and he answered within the first few rings.

"Alexus, you okay?" he asked quickly.

"I'm fine, I'm at my mother's. Where is Troy?" I said as I rubbed my stomach.

"At my house, sleeping in the guest room, I think. Things have been said that didn't sit well with him." He told me, a hint of sadness in his voice.

"How is he holdin' up?" I asked, standing up and slipping on my shoes.

"He's been crying for the most part and asking for you." He informed me, which made me feel even worse for ignoring him. "I never seen him like this, ever." I nodded and knew it was bad.

"I'm on my way." I told him quietly before hanging up.

Even though I was upset with him for hanging up on me and leaving me in the dark, I couldn't leave him alone. Knowing he was crying in front of people other than me, let me know he was hurt. Troy never cried, he held in all his emotions.

"Troy." I pushed open the room door softly, being welcomed to darkness.

I heard him sniffle, and as soon as I laid down next to him, he wrapped himself around me. I sighed, and ran my hand through his soft curls, pecking his lips repeatedly.

"Talk to me, please." I whispered, rubbing his shoulder.

"Tthey tryna tell me she not my real momma, Lex. How they gon' tell me that?" he cried. I sighed deeply as I turned his face to mine.

"Don't take that to heart, Troy. Okay? They're just trying to get you down, baby." I said putting my hand on the side of his face. Wiping away some of his tears. "You're strong. I've never seen you cry except..." He nodded and buried his head into my neck.

"But what if the woman that's six feet under, that I loved so much, isn't my momma? How can anyone lie like that? Do their son that way?! I had to hear that for two men, already. They're saying Melina is my mom! Melina, Alexus! I don't know that woman. How is she my moms?" He said getting angry.

"Baby, calm down. Just relax. Maybe you need to talk to your dad." He shot up and glare at me.

"I don't have shit to say to him! All he has done to me is lie and treat me like shit! If I go over there, it's to go through my mom's stuff so I can find something out myself. I don't know what I'll do if..."

"Don't say stuff like that! Just sleep it off okay?" He looked at me and I could tell how angry he truly was.

"Tell me what happened, today." He looked away from me and I knew it we something terrible.

"Troy?" I pleaded.

"Just let it go. You don't need to know about any of that. Just lay on me, please?" I nodded and crawled on top of him.

"T-Troy? Did you, k..." I stammered before he cut me off.

"I did it cause I had to baby. I'm telling you when our baby comes, I'm out the game." I nodded against his chest and dropped the entire conversation. I didn't want to talk about this anyway. I rubbed my stomach as he ran his hands through my hair with one hand and rubbed my booty with the other.

"I hope you will." I whispered as I drifted off to sleep. I needed him safe and home with me. I didn't want him doing this for a living anymore.

Monet Dragun

Chapter Eleven
Troy

I woke up this morning angry. I was angry at the fact that Denise Griffin is possibly not my birth mother. It hurt me deep inside and I had to find out answers. "I'm about to go, Lex." I said as I pulled my shirt over my head. She sat up and stared at me.

"Don't let it get to you okay?" I sighed and ran my hand down my face. I slipped my sunglasses on my face and proceed to the door, but her sultry sweet voice stopped me in my tracks.

"Troy, please?" I sighed again as I turned to look at her.

"Please, what, Alexus? I'm going to be cool about the whole ordeal, okay? Just have some faith in me damn." I said it harsher than I intended on doing when I seen those big brown eyes about to cry. "Babe, I'm sorry. It's just I got a lot going through my head, okay? I'll call you later. I swear I won't do nothing out of pocket, I promise, okay?" She just nodded and fiddled with my fingers as she looked at me. Walking over to her I pecked her forehead.

"Love you." I said trailing off. She planted a soft kiss on my cheek.

"Love you too. Don't let it get to you, okay?" I nodded and grabbed my phone plus my keys. I made my way out of the room and to my car. A lot more than a lot was going through my head.

What if I find something I shouldn't?

What if Melina is my mom?

What if I actually am adopted?

All these "what if" questions ran through my mind as I pulled out of Marcus' driveway. I didn't let my father know I was coming over. I didn't even want to speak to him. I just wanted to find out my own answers. I needed to know. Maybe my mom left me something. Something to tell me who I really was and where I really came from. I needed to know. Maybe I needed to get in contact with Melina. How on earth was I to do that, though? The first time I met her, she smiled in my face like I meant nothing to her, like she just had met me.

I don't know how I was going to react when I seen my father, so I decided to just get in and out of there. I didn't want to be probed with question after question. I just needed my head cleared. I couldn't keep going on like this.

***

Pulling into my dad's gravel driveway, I put my car in park and took out my keys. Getting out, I took a long deep breath and locked up my car. I adjusted my sunglasses as I walked up the small steps. I knocked in the door and scratched the back of my neck waiting for someone to open it. "C'mon." I said to myself as I knocked again.

I heard shuffling on the other end and footsteps shuffling towards the door. "Who is it?" The woman asked.

"It's Troy." I stated as I shoved my hands into my pockets. The door quickly unlocked, and my eyes met with Melina's. Awh shit, I wasn't expecting to see her here.

"Hello, Troy. Come in, come in. It's a little nippy out there." I nodded and came in as she locked the door.

"Thought you were done with my father?" She sighed and motioned me to sit on the plush sofa next to her.

"I am, but he needed someone to take care of him. I just have a big heart, so I'm helping him out 'round the house. What brings you over here? I haven't heard from you since I seen you at the hospital." She said as she picked up her coffee mug. I nodded and ran my hand down my face.

"I just came over here to get some of my mom's stuff out of her study. Uh, some things were said, and I just need some answers." I said as I trailed off and looked away avoided her death stare.

"Well, her room hasn't been touched. Yyou can go up there if you'd like. I won't hold you up." She said giving me a genuine smile.

"Melina, I hav" I was cut off when he walked into the room. My jaw immediately tensed up and my fist balled up. Melina

77

must've noticed because she rubbed my leg. Something my mom would do to calm me down.

"Son! Long time no see. What bring..." I cut him off. I didn't want to hear his fake lines.

"I'm not hear for small talk, okay? I just came to get some of my mother's things if you don't mind. Melina, it was nice talking to you again." I got up and walked straight past my father and up the staircase. My heart rate picked up as I neared my mom's study. It seemed like the hallway was getting smaller and smaller. My palms began to sweat as I grabbed the knob of the door. "Just relax, Troy." I inhaled then exhaled. I opened the door and walked in. Her scent still lingered in the room. Her ever so sweet peach splash perfume lingered.

I smiled as I looked at everything still in its place. I looked at where I could start at, so I decided to start at her desk. The old cherry Apple wood desktop was smooth to the touch. It was a little dusty here and there. I didn't want to mess up how she had her things set up, but something told me to open her desk drawer.

So, I did. I opened it slowly and looked at her old letters. I shuffled through them and came across and thick envelope with my name on it. "What is this?" I picked it up and fiddled with it. Debating if I should open it or not. "Mom, what are you trying to tell me, man?" I took off my sunglasses and rubbed my eyes. I was so flustered. I didn't know what to do. So, I stuffed the letter into my back pocket.

I turned around to my father staring at me. "I loved when she sat in that seat and wrote her stories. Troy, I really loved your Mom. I miss her as much as you do." I chuckled and shook my head. I was fuming inside.

"Oh, you loved her?! You loved her! If you loved her so much, then why isn't she here huh? Why isn't she still sitting here, gahdammit!" I shouted. My face was hot, and I was squeezing my fist so hard, I could feel my nails piercing my skin.

"Troy, do not curse in my house! Your mom and I had our differences, but..."

"But what! Is she my real mom? Is she!" I licked my dry lips as I stared at him. He became silent so I asked again."Is SHE my real mom! The one I mourned over since I was sixteenyearsold!" I shouted more harsher than I intended.

"Troy, you just don't understand okay?"

I don't understand! Me, I don't understand." I began to pace, and more fuel was added to this fire when I heard that bastards voice.

"Sup, pops oh, if it isn't momma's boy?" He chuckled. After he said that, I was seeing red. I wanted to kill Stephen.

"Ion' think you wanna say shit to me, Stephen. I'll fuck your ass up right here and now! Don't try me!" I pushed past them both and made my way downstairs. Melina was crying and I wanted to ask why. I guess she heard me and my dad's conservation.

I shrugged and walked towards the door before she called out my name. "TTroy?" I still didn't turn around. "TTroy, please?"

"What, Melina?"

"I was yyoung and I didn't..."

"You what?! You ain't want me?! I wasn't good enough for you or somethin'?!" I snapped at her, as she flinched.

"Troy you need to..." My father began, coming down the stairs.

"You need ta' shut the fuck up!" I yelled. "Y'all ain't nothing but a bunch of fuckin' liars!"

"You're my son. I llove you." Melina cried, standing up.

I laughed and shook my head. "I ain't shit to y'all. None of y'all twisted muh'fucka's will ever know what love is. I'm out! Don't call nor text me! I ain't shit to y'all." I stormed out the house making sure to slam the door. Making my way over to the car, I hopped in and slammed the door. I slammed my hands repeatedly on the steering wheel and shouted as angry tears streamed down my face.

I gripped the envelope, and all my answers are right here in the envelope. I'm just so scared to see it. My whole life has been a lie. I peeled out of the driveway and didn't look back. I couldn't fathom what was going on in my life and I wanted all of this to be dealt with. But I didn't know how to do it.

***

Stephen

After that little family incident, I went off to see about Ciara. I knew she was at the modeling agency. She should've known it was only a matter of time before I was going by to see her.

I fixed my chain and shirt as I got out of my truck. I made my way towards the entrance and opened the door. "Hello, sir. How may I help you?" I nodded.

"Yeah, I need to see Ciara. I miss my girl it'll only take a second." She was hesitant for a moment but nodded her head.

"She's in her office sir, and your name is Marcus, right?" She questioned.

"Yep, in the flesh." I smirked. She gave me a pass and I gave her a smiled as I walked off. She just doesn't know what she caused.

I knocked on the door and her sweet loud voice answered back. "Come in! If it's Sarah, I need those photos for the sh Stephen? What are you doing here?!" She said as she backed away knocking over some things on her desk as she tried to escape.

I closed the door and locked it. "So, you think you just gon' leave me like that? Huh? You think it's that damn easy!" I shouted causing her to jump in fear.

"You cheated countless times! And you expected me to stay and go through that pain!" She yelled back. I laughed darkly as my hand made it around her neck.

"So? You cheat and get pregnant by that nigga! Nah it doesn't work that way! You gon' pay, you feel me?" She scratched at my hand and I crashed my lips into hers.

"Get out! Mar…"

"He ain't gone do shit! And if you tell, just know I'ma kill him and that damn bastard baby of yours! Now, open your gah'damn legs CiCi! You know you always liked it rough." I chuckled. She tried so hard to fight back, but I was to strong. I was going to ruin Marcus and Troy by targeting their most precious loved ones. They never seen it coming.

I unbuckled my pants and she slapped me. "Bitch!" I slapped her and ripped her panties off before pushing my member inside. "I'm the best thing that ever happened to you. Now take it!"

Chapter Twelve
Marcus

Sometimes I wonder, how I keep on goin' on
I love the weed, blow that odor
You smell the loud, that's my cologne, yeah baby
Sometimes I wonder, where these niggas goin' wrong
I'm a young ass nigga, but I could buy your bitch a home, yeah baby

I stopped Fetty Wap's *I Wonder* as I heard Ciara come in the house. I put my phone down and look at the hallway as I waited for her to come around the corner.

"Hey, babe how was your day?" I asked as my phone buzzed.

I was texting Lex. She said Troy hadn't texted or called her yet and she's a bit worried. That was indeed weird for him. It was eleven something at night, and she said he hasn't even made it home yet. She told me about how he went over to his father's house to get some of his "mom's" things. In my opinion, I know something went wrong.

"It was fine." Ciara whispered, but I could barely hear a word she said, as she put down her keys and purse. She wasn't as perky as she usually was. This wasn't like the CiCi I knew.

"Let me go check on, Sophia. I'll be right back." I tossed my phone on the couch cushion as I got up and pulled up my saggy sweatpants.

Ciara didn't make eye contact when I looked at her and I knew something was off. I just shrugged it off and went upstairs to check up on Phia.

I softly walked up the stairs. As I walked into her bedroom that I was getting decorated, I saw she was still laying sprawled out on the bed with her stuffed animals surrounding her. I smiled and kissed her cheek as she snored lightly in her sleep. She was so adorable.

"Sleep well, daddy's baby." I said smiling as I made my way out of her room, slightly closing the door.

When I was walking down the steps, I heard sniffling and muffled groans and moans. Scrunching up my face I quickened my speed down the stairs and was met with a Ciara who was crying her eyes out.

"Baby? What's the matter? You didn't get the gig or something?" I said completely baffled.

She violently shook her head.

"HHe" she bursted into even more tears as her words got caught in her throat. He who?

"Who, baby? Talk to me? Please." I said as I sat next to her and pulled her into my lap.

"Marcus, I... I tried to stop him. I swear." She cried into my chest. Who was she talking about? What got her this way? Who been fucking with my baby!

"Who hurt you CiCi? Who exactly hurt you? You can tell me. I won't overreact. I promise." That part I lied about. I shifted in my seat, squeezing her tighter. Trying to get her attention, she was so spaced out.

"I'm sorry, Marcus, but, I can't. It nothing. Just the job is stressful and its that time of the month." Was all she needed to cry to let me know he, whoever he was, had done something. She tried to play it off, but I knew all to well.

I moved her off me and stood up quickly and walked over to the cabinet where I kept another one of my guns. I made sure it was loaded before I slipped it into my waistband. As soon as my hand got a grasp on the doorknob, I heard Ciara call my name.

"Can you jjust stay with me tonight? I'm scared. It's nothing babe, really." She mumbled, wiping away her tears.

I nodded and licked my lips as I put the gun back in the cabinet. I couldn't find the right words to even speak. My blood was boiling, and my nerves were beyond bad. I just wanted to get my hands on that nigga. I knew it was more to Ciara's story that she wasn't telling me.

I tried my hardest to tolerate him as much as I could only for the simple fact, he was related Troy. Even though plenty of times before, Troy said he wasn't his brother. There was a certain line you don't cross with me and mine, and he had crossed it.

"I love you, Marcus." Ciara whispered into my chest as she began to slow her crying down.

"I love you too." I said honestly, as I ran my hand through her short hair. I had to get this shit figured out, Ciara been through too much with that wack ass nigga. I had to do right by shorty no way was I about to lose her ever again.

***

Troy

"Remember that one time you were makin' me my favorite after a football game momma? I tried ta' open up the pot and you slapped my hand away, so I called Nana, and she said, 'you betta' not hit ma' football star Denise!'" I laughed, leaning against my mother's stone.

I had been here ever since I left my dad's house, or should I say Curtis' house. I'd been venting to her and reminiscing on old stories we had shared together for hours. I turned off my phone and got everything I had to say off my chest.

I turned on my phone and saw that time had passed by. It was now nearing twelve in the morning. I knew it was night because of the darkness, I just didn't expect it to be this late.

Text messages and missed phone calls from Lex, Marcus, as well as a few from Curtis and Melina started to roll in. I sighed, knowing Lex was probably worried sick.

"Momma, I think I needa get goin' now. It was nice talkin' to you. I know I don't come here as often as I should, but I'ma start, I promise." I kissed the stone and patted it. "Like I said earlier momma, ain't nobody takin' yo' place. I don't care what they say. You raised me and loved me, so you're my momma and I love you wit' all of my heart."

I quickly glanced down at the small engraved picture of her on the stone before walking away. Tears were burning in my eyes and I didn't want to cry again.

I got into my car and began the small drive home. It was a quick drive, and as soon as I pulled up, I could see the downstairs light flicked on.

I opened the door and Lex was pacing back and forth, hysterical, texting away.

"Baby?" I called out to get her attention.

She dropped her phone and ran over to me, wrapping her legs around my waist and kissing my lips repeatedly. As soon as I dropped her, she hit my chest and wiped her tears.

"You scared me Troy!" she yelled. "I thought something happened to you!"

"I'm sorry Lex. I just had ta' visit my momma and get some things off of ma' chest." I sighed, as she hugged me once more.

"You got the answers you were lookin' for?" she asked, with a small smile.

"Not really." I shrugged. "But it's okay."

She smiled at me and kissed my lips. "Wanna go lay down, Papi?"

I nodded my head as she led me into the bedroom. I kicked off my pants and slipped out of my shirt and hopped into the bed. Lex wrapped her small body around mine and played with my beard while I rubbed her back.

"Baby?" she whispered.

"Wassup?" I answered.

"I was readin' online with my mom that professional football teams take on free agents"

"No Lex." I cut her off, knowing exactly where she was going with this.

"But you said you wanted to get out the game, right?" she said.

"Yes, but I gave up football a long time ago after Stephen stole that dream." I replied with a sigh.

"And? Baby you have a talent and a drive for that sport. Teams would be begging for a guy like you on their team. All you have to do is a hire an agent and get him to do the rest." She begged.

I sighed, knowing I wasn't going to really do it. "I'll think about it."

"You will?" she perked up, causing me to chuckle.

"Yeah baby, I will." I said as I ran my hand along my face. She pulled my hand away from my face as it rested it there.

"Baby? What's the matter? Really. What did you find out today?" I sighed as I felt my blood boiling again. I held back my tears so hard. "Troy? Talk to me, please!" She got on top of me as she looked down on me.

"I found out some heavy shit today, Bae, she's not my real mom, Lex! Damn, mane' she not my momma, baby!" I sat up as I clung to her as I put my head on her stomach as she held onto my head.

"Who's not your mom?!" She said baffled and shocked.

"Denise! She's not my mom, but in a sense, she is, but she's not my biological mother." I bit my lips as I held in those tears.

"Who's your mom? Talk to me?" She said pulling my face away to look deep into my eyes.

"M-M-Melina! She my mom. Why didn't she want me Alexus, why?!"

"Shh, shh, shh, Troy! Don't do this to yourself, Papi!" She wiped away my stray tear. I told her to grab my jeans that I had on today.

"Okay, what do you need?" I sighed deeply.

"Get the thick envelope from my back pocket. It's from my mom to me. I'm so damn scared to read it. Can yyou please read it, Lex? I need you right now." She nodded and stuck her long nail in the crease. She tore it from the side and pulled the tan papers put.

"You sure you want to hear it now?" I nodded and laid back looking at her.

"I'm very sure." She nodded and unfolded it.

"Okay, love.

Dear Peanut,

I have something to tell you. Actually, a lot love. I'm so sorry that you've been through pure hell. Don't worry that word is in the bible. You're the love of my life Troy. My little Trojan solider. Stephen can be a handful and I know he does a lot to make you feel unwanted. But, baby boy, you're special and I always told you, don't let no one change you. Make them take you as you are. And I want you to take that to heart, Troy!

But the point I'm trying to get to get to is that, I'm not your biological mother and son, that reason is because of your "father" had his terrible ways, Troy. I wanted you to be mine. Your real mother wasn't ready to be a mother. She didn't want to abandon you, but Curtis was so damn stubborn. Son, that's also in the bible. I never wanted you to go through this, son. You are a child of the Lord and don't forget it, okay? Don't let Stephen, your father, or Melina break your precious heart, okay? Promise me that?

And, Troy, some horrible people are really out there. Because of that some bad things have happened. I didn't die from a broken heart and I'm telling you this because I know I'm going to leave this earth soon. It's my time son. This is something from your father's past. Before he became a preacher, he hasn't paid his dues, so his enemy will take something most important to him. This is what he will do. They will kill me and take my life from you. I can feel it. Curtis won't believe it, but my exhusband before your father, they were friends. The keyword is were.

He wanted revenge. Revenge on him for taking me. He was once abusive, and that's where Curtis swooped me up and saved me. Curtis won't believe me though and this is the real reason why I am no longer on this earth. I love you with all my heart and don't forget that. Don't be so hard on Melina. Please, son. I don't have time left. Don't take this out on your father. It won't solve anything, and it won't bring me back, son. That's the honest to God truth. I'm in Gods hands now. And Troy I'm always with you.

love, mommy Denise

After, Lex got done reading, she was in tears and I was on a mission to find and kill this man who did this to my mother. My father is dead to me to the hundredth power.

"Troy, I'm so sorry. Come here." She laid the papers down and hugged me tight.

I had no emotions, and I couldn't speak. I was in another world. I couldn't believe this madness. "Alexus, I'ma need for you to call that agent soon." That was all I could say. She just looked at me and nodded. She knew me, and she knew I was highly upset.

"Okay, Troy." I rubbed her stomach and kissed it multiple times.

"My son or daughter will never have to go through this bullshit!" I said out of rage. She grabbed my face and kissed me and didn't plan on letting go. I could feel my body heat relaxing. Lex knew how to care for me and calm me down. I'm glad for that because I would've murdered someone by now.

And I will be murdering someone soon.

Chapter Thirteen
Troy
Three Weeks Later...

"Troy, what should we name the baby?" Lex questioned out of the blue.

I sat on one end of the couch and she sat on the other side of me with her legs in my lap as I rubbed her feet.

"I mean in all honesty, I don't know babe. But if it's a girl," I paused. "I'd love if we name her Denise or have it as her middle name." I said trailing off.

She looked at me intensively and fiddled with her fingers.

"I love that idea. I have no problem with naming the baby after her." She said as she finally spoke up. I gave her a small smile and continued rubbing her feet. "But, if it's a boy, I'd like the name Hector."

She laughed and shook her head. "You and that movie, Troy. But of course."

"What?" I questioned.

"You and this damn Greek mythology is going to be the death of me, Troy." She shook her head.

I shrugged and chuckled simultaneously. "You know ya' nigga smart, but I like that name. It's strong and says something."

She nodded. "Yeah, you have a point there. I like it too." She puckered her lips, and I shook my head at her silliness. I leaned closer to her and pecked her lips. When I pulled away, she looked at me deep into my eyes as if she was searching for something. She was staring into my soul.

"What, Lex?" I inquired, she sighed deeply and gave me a face of heartbreak.

"Ciara, told me something a few days ago and..." a hardstrong knock pulled me away from her conversation.

"Hold that thought babe, okay?" I told her

She sighed and nodded. She moved her legs and rubbed her stomach in small circles. She was slowly showing each day.

The knocking continued as I neared the door. Looking through the peep pole, it was none other than Marcus. I opened it and gave him a brotherly hug.

"S'up, my nigga? Why the hell are you banging on my door like you the police!" I said as I invited him in. I haven't spoke or seen Marcus in three weeks.

He laughed, "Man, this was something I just couldn't talk about over the phone." Marcus waltzed in as I closed the door. He began pacing my wooden floors. He had bags under his eyes, his hair was nappy, and his facial hair was out of control. Not to mention his damn breath was on ten. He looked as if he hadn't had sleep in a long time.

"Man, chill. What's wrong? Over here looking like a mountain man." I said putting my hands on his shoulders.

"That's the thing! I don't know what's wrong. Ciara. Man, Ciara, she's been crying a lot lately. She's been off the game man. I've never seen her down like this! About a few weeks ago, she came home and was crying saying, 'I didn't mean for him to do it.' I still don't know who 'him' is! Troy, I'm out of my mind! I have a feeling someone hurt my baby! I swear I'ma kill him if I find out who he is!" He yelled causing Lex to jump. Her eyes were wide at Marcus' hysterics.

"Baby, I'm going upstairs. Please, keep it down a little. I don't need the stress, neither do you." She nodded and scurried up the stairs to our room.

"Sorry, baby girl!" He yelled, then she yelled back making me shake my head.

"It's okay, big head Marcus!"

"I'm sorry for the outburst. It's just I need to know. She's never been this way. Someone did something to her." I nodded, and we both sat down at the table. I've known Ciara for awhile and she's never been trouble. Everyone always loved her just like Alexus. The only person I could think of hurting her was Stephen, but he couldn't be entirely that damn crazy.

"We'll find out who did it and we'll find out who killed my momma too." I blurted out. His eyes widened and he parted his lips to speak, but I just waved him off for him to stop. "I don't want to explain, okay? Just know we out for two people." He nodded. There was a deep pause before he spoke again.

"I think Stephen got something to do with this. I can feel it bro. He's the only one that would want to hurt her." He said balling up his fist.

"I'ma call 'round because she like my sister and I wouldn't want anything to happen to her, just like you'd look out for Lex." He nodded and scratched his beard.

"But in all honesty, your brother gotta go. I'm ready for his ass to be six feet unda'." I shivered at the fact that he called Stephen my brother.

"That ain't my brother. Melina is my real momma." His eyes widened and he put his hand on my shoulder.

"Man! I'm sorry to hear that. Denise was the best man, but who is Melina? Catch me up bruh." As I was about to tell him, Lex came down.

"Babe!" She whined as she came down the steps with her phone in her hand. "Can we go out tonight, like a dinner date? Like all four of us?" She pouted. I smiled at her short pregnant self.

I waved her off. "Yeah Bae, we can. But me and Marcus is having an important talk okay?" She nodded and skipped away upstairs with the phone pressed against her ear. That must've been Ciara.

"Anyways, she uh, she was young and left me wit' my pops and he pushed me onto Denise. So, technically Melina is my biological mother, but Denise." I smiled at the thought of her, "That's my momma."

Marcus nodded and dapped me up. "I understand bruh. Aye, you serious about this dinner date?"

I laughed and nodded. "Can't say no ta' a pregnant lady. Go get ready bruh."

"But wait, about this killin' the person who killed yo' momma, explain." he raised an eyebrow.

I didn't feel like talking about my discovery just yet. It still hurt a lot, but it was something Marcus needed to know. Instead, I retrieved the letter my momma had written it to me and handed it over to him. He read it and his facial expressions had changed a bunch. They went from sad ones, to angry ones, even a few smiles.

"Denise sure as hell loved that bible." he laughed.

I nodded with a small smile. "But aye, you down? I want that nigga's head, whoever he is."

"You know I'm down for you my brotha'."

***

"So, what do you guys want? A boy or a girl?" Ciara asked, as she leaned on Marcus' shoulder.

"I'm torn. I want a girl so I can dress her in all those cute clothes, but then I want a boy so he could be my mini Troy." Lex pouted, looking up at me.

"Boy." I replied quickly. "Y'all girls, see y'all built wit' too much, and I'm equipped ta' kill a nigga over my baby girl. Wspecially if her body fills out like Lex over here. Ya feel me?" She nudged my side with a slight giggle, knowing she was thick as Serena Willams.

"I feel ya!" Marcus laughed, dapping me up across the table.

"You guys are so annoying." Ciara shook her head at the both of us causing Lex to roll her eyes as well.

"Nah, I'm just fuckin' around. Just as long as my baby come out healthy, wit' some strong athletics and smarts like they Momma, I'll be happy." I smiled, looking down at a cheesy Lex.

"You're so cute baby." Lex pecked my cheek, rubbing her hand up and down my arm.

Marcus cleared his throat, which caused us to look up at him. His eyes moved towards the direction of Ciara, who had tears in hers. I furrowed my eyebrows and turned towards where she was looking at.

Stephen. He walked into the restaurant with a female attached to his arm and a wide smile plastered on his face.

"Tell him Ci." Lex whispered, touching her hand.

"Tell me what?" Marcus asked, furrowing his brows.

Ciara just shook her head and wiped the tears that were beginning to fall.

"Lex. If you know something, speak up and speak up now. I'm not playing with you." I growled, feeling my fist ball up.

Alexus looked over at Ciara, who's face was in Marcus' chest, silently sobbing.

"H-he told the lady at the front desk that he was Mar." she said lowly, "And hhe went back there and raped her Troy."

My blood immediately began to boil. I knew Stephen was dirty, and a piece of shit, but I never expected him to go that low. Rape was an ultimate form of disrespect and disgust, and of course, he had reached that low.

I could only imagine if somebody did that to Lex.

I looked over at Marcus who was consoling Ciara. "Aye, you said you wanted to kill that nigga?"

Marcus just looked up at me, knowing I knew what went down, and nodded. My fingers started to tap furiously on the table and my jaw began to twitch.

"Let's go." I said sternly.

"Please, not here Troy. We were having a good time." Lex whispered, touching my arm.

"How we supposed to have a good time when the nigga that raped Ciara is sittin' ova' there cuttin' it up?! Like he ain't did a damn thing!" I snapped at her, as she jumped. "I just called you smart! Use ya' fuckin' brain Alexus, don't be fucking stupid!" I yelled out of anger.

"I just…"

"Shut up, Lex! Damn, stop bein' selfish and let us take care of our shit!" I slammed my fist down, as she quickly looked away.

She looked down and played with her fingers, nodding.

"Troy, she gotta point. This place a lil' crowded." Marcus commented. "Let's just go, and we could do a lil' stake out when he goes to Curtis' house."

I bit my lip and nodded, "A'ight."

Marcus and I both threw a few hundreds on the table and walked away. Ciara was clinging to his side. "Babe, tthat was the receptionist at my job." She said lowly. I shook my head and looked back to see Lex, as she trailed behind me.

"Baby, I'm sorry." I turned around, as I heard her sniffling.

"It's okay." She smiled small and got inside the car before resting her head against the window and pulling down her skirt.

I sighed and shook my head, knowing I fucked up. Lex was always sensitive, but now that she's pregnant? Any wrong move would make her bust out in tears. Yelling at her and calling her stupid was a wrong move.

"Lex, I ain't mean" Again, she cut me off.

"It's okay. It was stupid of me to try to stop you, Troy. And I was being selfish. Can we just go home? I'm really tired." She trailed off, something she did when she was usually upset.

I ran my hand down my face and nodded, turning on the car and driving home. As soon as we got there, Lex disappeared into our bedroom. I poured me a shot, and quickly threw it back, letting the burning sensation trickle down my throat.

"Alexus?" I called out as I entered the dark room.

Her face was hidden within the covers. I pulled them back a little bit and saw her tear stained cheeks. She had obviously cried herself to a quick slumber as soon as we got here. I immediately felt worse, the more I stared at her. I shouldn't have been so mean and hard on her. She didn't deserve that at all.

My phone buzzed in my pocket, and sure enough, it was a text from Marcus.

Marcus: Tomorrow morning at 8. Meet me at my crib and we'll drive over to Curtis'.

I sent him a quick text and put my phone down. I sighed quietly as I sat on the end of the bed. All I could think about was what Stephen did to Ciara and the fact that he waltzed in with another woman at that. The fact that she worked at her job was worse. I pulled off my shirt and pants and got in the bed. I pulled Lex close to me. I didn't want her mad at me.

***

The following morning, I woke up alone. I looked for my phone and grabbed it off the bed banister. The time read 7:01. I sighed and got up. I rubbed the sleep out of my eyes as I walked out of the room. The smell of breakfast cooking made me walk downstairs. Lex was in one of my shirts and cutting up some fruit. I walked up behind her and gently pulled her close to me.

"Morning, baby." I planted a kiss on her cheek. She didn't budge or smile that smile I loved so much. "Babe, I'm sorry for hurting your feelings like that last night. Really." I reassured her.

"Hi, Troy and it's fine. I made you breakfast." She didn't even look my way.

"Lex, it's not okay! I didn't mean to say that harsh shit. Just my brother and the Ciara thing." she put her hand up for me to stop talking and I did just that.

"I know how you feel about him, and the Ciara situation made it worse. It wasn't right for me to interfere. I accept your apology." She said giving me a small smile. But I knew she was still upset. I walked over to her and kiss her.

"I'ma make it up to you, but I have business to take care of. I can't be late." She nodded, no begging for me to stay. No kiss. No, no nothing. I'm really in trouble now. "I love you Lex."

"Love you, too." She didn't look at me. She just walked over to the couch and ate her food. God, help me.

***

Marcus

Me and Troy had just left my house and we were dressed all in black. I was determined to get this nigga.

"You sure he gone be going over ya' pops house at this time?" He nodded.

"Yep, he'll be coming around twelve at night and he thinks I don't know. I know exactly why, too." I looked over at him as I drove in my jeep.

96

"Why?" I questioned.

"Because since his debt isn't paid off, he's using my father. Even though I hate him right now, I can't let him run him dry." I nodded in agreement as we came to a halt.

"All we gotta do is grab him and drive him to the spot. No games, now Troy." He eyed me.

"I hate his ass, why would I ruin it? He hurt Ciara, hurt my family. He's dead to me, point blank period." I nodded and dapped him up.

"Brothers fa' life." He smiled.

"Yeah, mane'. Brothers fa' life."

Darkness fell and at about twelve exactly, Stephen's car pulled in. Me and Troy put our mask on and got out the car. I bit my bottom lip as I gripped my gun in my right hand as we jogged up towards him swiftly.

"What the fuck!" He yelped. I hit him with the butt end of my gun, and he fell out. "Marcus I'm about to get his ass up." Troy went to the drive side snatched the door open, pulled Stephen out of the car and threw him over his shoulder. Then with one hand fished his keys out his pocket. He tossed them to me, and I hopped in his car.

Troy tossed him in the back, and he jogged over to my jeep. I back out and waited for him to pull off first. This nigga was in for a rude awakening.

***

"Wake yo' bitch ass up!" I said as Troy threw ice cold water on him. He gasped and shook his head from side to side. "What's up big boy?" I said as I slapped his face.

"How ya' feeling brother?" Troy said as he stood in front of him with his hands crossing in front of him. His Rolex gleaming.

"Troy?! What the hell!" Stephen yelled.

"I'd suggest you keep ya' tone down yo'. So, you won't get ya' head knocked off." I said cracking my knuckles.

"Man! Let me the fuck go. I ain't do shit!" He screamed. Troy cracked his neck and spoke before me.

"You know what the fuck you did!" He yelled into his face.

He began to chuckle darkly. "Oh, you mean getting a piece of that cookie that Ciara got between her legs, huh? Shit was good br…" I began to hit him with fury punches. Troy didn't pull me back until he seen blood.

"Nah! I wanna kill his ass!" I spat.

"His time gone come. But right now, he gone suffer and we ain't about to get our hands dirty"

"Man! Her shit was good. She was screaming like the bitch she was for you!" Troy turned his way and adjusted his brass knuckles and cracked him in the face, knocking him out cold.

"Oh, his time gone come, Marcus. Believe that shit!" He fixed his clothes and called down Bucum and King.

"Handle his ass and make his ass wish he never did what he did to my baby girl!" They nodded at Troy's command and we both went up the steps of the house.

"Mane, I'm glad you got my back." He nodded.

"It ain't no thang. He got what the hell he was asking for. Now, we can both go home and fix things with our girls. Especially me." I nodded.

"So, when are we getting out the game?" I asked out the blue.

"When we find the man that killed my mother." He said bluntly and not even looking my way. There were no more words to say after that statement and I thought I had a grudge? I was going to kill Stephen. Well not exactly. Break his legs? Yes. Kill, him? Just a little bit. But Troy that was a whole 'nother ball game.

Monet Dragun

Chapter Fourteen
Troy

"So, what are we going to do with him? He needs to die." Marcus stated boldly as we sat in the car outside of his house.

Could I kill my own blood? I have no clue, but that nigga had done so much scandalous shit to me, it was a shame. "I don't know. That's still blood, even though I hate his ass." Marcus scoffed and slammed his hand on the dashboard.

"So, you just going to let this shit slide? The fuck kind of brother has he been to you? We're gone let him go after what he fucking did to Ciara? What if that was fucking Alexus, huh?! You'll be all up for killing him then, but since it's my girl you wanna let him go? What type of bullshît is that! I thought we were brothers. I've been there for you more than he's ever been there for you, yo'! This nigga raped Ciara! He beat her like she wasn't shit, violated my baby because he's sick and can't have what he once lost! He took her fucking trust and sprits with him! That's justified, son? Huh, Troy? Is it!" I deeply sighed. He had a point, and I was being soft.

"Marcus, bruh. It," he opened the door and slammed it, but before he left, he stuck his head through the window.

"Just know, he gon' come after Alexus next and when he does, how will you feel when I'm not on yo' side? Think about that. I'm gone." He turned around and made his way to the house.

"Marcus! Mar!" He didn't even look my way. I sighed deeply and pulled off. I'll just let him blow off his anger. I didn't even let Stephen go, and he's already blowing up on me. God, can you ever give me a break? Please.

***

"Baby! I'm home!" I yelled as I came into the house. Deep chills ran down my spine as I entered the house. I closed the door and looked around.

100

Nothing but silence filed the room was all I heard. I sighed and kicked off my shoes and made my way through the foyer as I went up the steps that lead up to the second floor of our home and then the bedroom. "Baby, you in here?" I said as I pushed the cracked door. She nodded and pointed to her phone as she sat up in the bed with it placed against her ear. I nodded and took off my jacket.

Her sweet Boston accent filled my ears. "Thanks, Ma. You are the best! I'll tell him right now. He just got here." She said as she said her goodbyes to her mom.

Raising an eyebrow, I had to ask. "What was that about?" I questioned.

"Well, she called up the agent and they'd like to meet you sometime soon." She shrugged with a slight attitude. Looked at her nails and kept eye contact away from me.

"Babe, are you still, you know, mad at me?" She shook her head no and continued to look at her phone. I walked over to her, and kissed her cheek multiple times. She scoffed and pushed me away. "Come on. If you not mad at me, then why are you turning your face up at me? Pushing me away from what's mine and crap? Babe, I said I was sorry. I ain't mean what I said. I hate when you do this." She mugged me and rolled her eyes.

"You always say shit on me with your angry! You say the hurtfulness shit, Troy! Do you know that? I've been with you since we were twelve years old, and you've always had fucking anger issues! You take your anger out on the ones that love you, and I am not about to stress out me and my baby! I'm here for you 24/7 and you know that!" I was in shock that she was talking like this. She was the more passive person ever. I can't believe I brought her out of her element like this.

"I was mad that you tried to sit me down like I was some lil' boy or somethin'. I ain't need you tryna' embarrass me in front of my boy." I shrugged, scratching the back of my neck.

"You cannot be serious," she laughed, throwing her hands down at her side. "Embarrass you, Troy? In front of Marcus? The most childish man on earth? Who's seen plenty of other embarrassing things out of you? Listen to how ridiculous you sound! I was trying to fucking protect you! I understand that you were angry about what he did to Ciara, believe me. I'm upset too, but we were in a fucking public place! With thousands of people who can fucking testify as witnesses, and what does that mean? They put you and Marcus away for a long fucking time and that means Sophia and our child no longer have their fathers." Alexus confessed in pure rage.

I watched a few tears spill from out of her eyes, but she quickly wiped them out of her eyes. It was almost like she didn't want to cry over me or the situation. "Plus, you had the audacity to call me stupid and selfish. Meanwhile, you were ready to just walk right out of your child's life and into a jail cell for a little bit of revenge." She scoffed and rolled her eyes once again. "I have done nothing but been here for you and support you. When you needed a shoulder to cry on, I was there! When you lost your mom, I was there! When your own fucking father talked down on you, I was there! What do I get in return? I get to hear how stupid and selfish I am. I get tired of all that lashing out you do towards me Troy. I swear I do." She said folding her arm over her chest.

I ran my hand down my face and sighed, I knew she was right. "I'm gonna…"

"Save it, Troy. I just need a little bit of time to cool off." She pulled her hair up into a ponytail.

I nodded my head. "I understand." I said while rubbing my beard. Lex threw me off, walked over to me, and pecked my lips, before running her small hands through my hair.

"And as angry as I am right now, Troy, whatever you do, whatever you're thinking of, please be smart about it. I love you with all my heart, and I couldn't bear the thought of losing you. You gotta be here to meet our baby. You made me a promise so keep that promise."

Lex grabbed my hands from my face and put my hand over her stomach with a smile. I nodded with certainty then pecked her stomach repeatedly. Lex softly pushed my head back and walked out of the room and made her way downstairs.

I laid back on the bed then stretched my hand out to pull out my phone, biting down on my bottom lip. Marcus was beyond pissed off at me, so I didn't want to call him. I probably needed to give him his time to cool off as well.

"Mr. Swiss." I mumbled to myself, pressing his name and calling.

"Helluh' Troy. Can I help ya'?" His raspy voice answered on the third ring.

"Yeah uhm, I need help findin' someone." I cleared my throat sitting up. "I figured since you tha' most powerful man in this city, you could help me."

"Who you need help findin'?" He asked.

"I don't know much about him except he killed my momma a few years back." I whispered, rubbing my knuckles.

"What's yo' mom's name, Troy?" he questioned.

"Denise, Denise Griffin. She was married to Curtis Griffin. He had his run ins with a few people, and they wanted to take something his family loved from him." I shook my head and took a deep breath in.

"Wait! Yo' father is Curtis Griffin?" The shock in Mr. Swiss' voice was apparent.

"Y-yeah?" I mumbled, almost embarrassed to be related to him.

"Curtis," he chuckled I shook my head in entire shame. "He had his pro'lems wit' Richie Rogers."

"Richie Rogers? Who is that?" I furrowed my 'brows in curiosity.

"Well yeah, Richie Rogers and him was always fightin'. Somethin' about Richie lil' sister bein' in love wit' him, and he was too busy tryna' steal Denise."

"Richie had a sister?" I scrunched up my face.

"Yeah. Melinda, Malia, Matilda…"

"Melina?" I cut him off annoyed.

"Yeah dat's ha'. Melina Rogers." He informed me.

I felt my heart drop to the pit of my stomach and my blood boil. "Thank you for yo' help, Mr. Swiss."

"It ain't a problem." He told me, before hanging up. I tossed my phone on the side of me and ran both of my hands down my face. What more could happen in my life? I needed a serious stress reliever. I needed Lex. I picked up my phone and still debated if I should message Marcus, but I didn't. I knew he was pissed about the whole Stephen thing. I got up with all my energy and walked out of the room.

Please, don't reject me Lex.,

That's all I thought in my head as I jogged down the steps. She was sitting on the couch Indian style and reading.

"B-baby?" I said as I looked at her with a long face. She took a double look at me and pulled her glasses off.

"What's the matter?" She said with a sigh.

"I-I just need you baby. Baby, I'm so sorry for hurting you, I swear. You're right I shouldn't take anything out on you." I said walking over to her and kneeling in front of her.

"Baby, I said you're good. You just needed to know." I cut her off by kissing her.

"Baby! Don't justify my actions. I was wrong and I want to make it up to you, can I please?" I begged. She pecked my lips twice before she spoke.

"Yes, you can, Papi." That's all I needed to hear. I picked her up as she wrapped her legs around my waist. This is what the fuck I needed. I needed my girl to satisfy me. Fuck a blunt and a drank, I needed her.

***

Marcus

"Ciara!" I called out as I rocked Sophia. She came down the stairs and smiled at me.

"Yes?" I handed her a sleeping Sophia and didn't make eye contact with her. "Mar."

"Please, don't okay? You told Alexus, but you didn't tell your own man what the nigga did to you?" I stressed.

"Please, she's sleep. Don't do this right now." I sighed and nodded. She took my baby girl upstairs and later came down with a sad face.

"Babe, let me explain please." I shrugged.

"I'm listening, speak." Tears fell down her eyes and she shook her head. "Stop crying please." I tried to confront her.

"Well, h-he. He came in my office and said he was going to hurt the ones you and Troy love. I didn't tell Alexus this part because of her baby. He said he was going to hurt Sophia, Marcus! I'm so-so sorry for not telling you."

"He threatened my child, and you don't tell me?! He put Lex and Troy in it knowing Lex is pregnant? Baby you told her and not me? How does that make me feel?" I said shooting up from the couch.

"Because he said he'll kill you! I can't lose you!" She yelled. I grabbed her and pulled her up making her look at me.

"You listen! He ain't gone do a goddamn thing to me! I'll kill his ass before he even tries to come near my family and that includes Troy and Lex! You hear me? I..." My phone began to ring, and she nodded for me to answer. I picked up the phone and answers it.

"What?!" I said harshly.

"Sorry, for bothering you but we have a situation." He stressed.

"What kind?" I said pacing.

"This Stephen nigga saying that if you don't talk to him now or let him go, he's going to have some nigga name Richie kill someone y'all love. I think he said her name was Melina." And at that very moment I knew I had to call Troy.

"A'ight. Knock his ass out! We'll be there soon." I hung up and looked at Ciara.

"Baby, I ain't mad. You gotta trust me and tell me things, okay? I ain't leaving you or Sophia. I love y'all. Y'all my family. But I gotta handle business. Get me..."

"Here." She handed me my gun and I didn't even know she went and got. "Take care of his ass. The world doesn't need that sick bastard alive." I never heard her talk this way and I knew she was my ride or die.

I had to hurry and call Troy, Stephen has gone way too far.

Monet Dragun

Chapter Fifteen

Troy

"Babe, can you stop real quick? My phone is ringing." I groaned as Lex moved up and down on me.

"Why!" She whined out of annoyance and pleasure. "I'm cutting you off, Troy. I swear. A pregnant woman has needs too." She huffed and handed well slammed my phone into my hand.

"We been making up for hours. You gotta chill, babe." I chuckled.

"Shut up, I have to go pee." She got up from the bed and her walk was all off. That's what the good pipe does to ya'. I groaned as my phone vibrated in my hands again. Now, he wants to talk to me.

I wasn't about to be petty. It might have been important.

"S'up?" I answered. But was quickly met with a panicked voice. "Yo' calm down?! What you mean?" I leaned up as I was trying to get a better understanding of the situation.

"Stephen, threatening your mama and something about a man named Richie." I felt instantly sick to my stomach. I shot up from the bed and looked around for my boxers.

"Shit. Shit. Shit!" I yelled into the phone. Nearly tripping over my own two feet. "I'll be there in five!" I hung up before he could get any words in. This was major. Too damn major.

"Babe? You okay in here?" Lex asked as she peeked into the room.

"No! It's some serious business I must go handle. It's a..." she cut me off by planting a kiss on my lips.

"I know, be careful and your gun is in its usual place! It's loaded!" She yelled as her naked body disappeared into the bathroom again. I was sort of baffled. No, begging me to stay? No, nothing? She loved the hell out of me.

"Lex!" She poked her head out with her eyebrows raised.

"Hmm?" She hummed.

"I love you girl." She smiled.

"Love you too. Now, go, Mr. Griffin you have bi'ness to deal with. My and my baby will be fine. Go, go!" This girl just doesn't know how she makes me feel. She was down for me.

***

As the gate opened and I drove into the facility, I could hear cursing and almost bones cracking. "Son of bitch! Who is Richie?!" *Smack!*

"Go to hell, Marcus!" Stephen spat in his face. Literally spit in his face as I came into the big and dark basement.

"What? You nas…" I held his fist back and pulled out my gun. The fun and games were over. Marcus was right, he didn't deserve to live for what he did to Ciara, and he don't deserve to live for associating with the man who killed my mother.

"You talk to the man who killed your own mom! The woman who gave birth to you?! You a cold sick son of a bitch!" I smacked him in the face with the gun, blood splattered all over the place.

"You bring our dad into this!"

Smack!

Smack!

I hit him with the one two's and watched as he gasped for air and spat out more blood.

"What you gotta say huh!? Huh?" I cocked the gun and he looked at me with swollen eyes. I didn't even see an ounce of remorse and a small smile appeared on his face.

"All I gotta say is, how's the baby doing?" He said with a chuckle as his coughed hard and spit up some more blood. My blood began to boil, and my index finger pulled the trigger, shooting him directly in the foot.

A piercing scream shot out of his mouth. And he groaned in agony. "Stephen, we're not brothers and I've came to terms with that. Now, you better talk and tell me about this nigga Richie, or I'll shoot you somewhere worse than that! Maybe, ya' dick since you used it to rape Ciara!" Marcus grabbed my arm and looked at me.

"We don't want to kill him yet and, I wanna know who this Richie dude is too and why he kill ya' moms." He mumbled into my ear.

I sighed and shrugged. "A'ight Stephen. You need to talk. You feel me? What's this shit about Richie?! Huh?" He took slow breaths and looked up at me with low eyes.

"Because you should check out who you call ya' fam. Melina ain't too sweet either and, once again, how's Alexus and the baby?" He probed with a smart mouth.

I furrowed my eyebrows and placed the tip of my gun to his forehead, "You tryna tell me something Stephen?"

He laughed and spit out the blood that was forming in his mouth, "I ain't sayin' shit."

I looked over at Marcus who was stroking his beard. "Call Alexus bruh."

Marcus nodded and pulled out his phone, dialing her number. After a few seconds he shook his head and tried again.

"She ain't answerin'." he sighed.

I looked over at Stephen who wore a smug look on his face. "Trouble in paradise?"

"I swea', let anything happen bad happen to my babies, and that's yo' life. I don't give a fuck what nobody says, ya heard me?" I growled through gritted teeth. "And I'll make sure you die slow."

***

Lex

"Mary had a little lamb, little lamb, little lamb," I sang to my stomach, rubbing it in circles. "Mary had a little lamb whose fleece was white as snow." I stopped to listen when I heard heavy footsteps dragging up the stairs, ceasing my singing. I stood up and stretched, admiring my small stomach.

"Daddy's back already peanut." I sang excitedly. "Maybe he'll take us to get some ice cream!" I heard someone approach the door.

I stepped out of the room door to come face to face with a tall man. He was muscular, and older, but definitely wasn't Troy.

I jumped back quickly, trying to get back into the room. The man's strong hand gripped me up quickly and slammed me against the wall.

"Boy or girl?" he chuckled evilly, staring me in my eyes.

I blinked quickly, feeling tears stream down my face, "P-please, don't hurt my baby. You can take whatever you want, the money, the jewelry, anything you want." I said scared out of my wits.

He laughed and dropped me, letting me slide down the wall. "I don't want yo' fuckin' money, Alexus. I want revenge."

"I d-didn't do anything." I said in a shaky voice.

"When you are in a relationship wit' Troy, you do enough." he laughed.

Before I could gather up my thoughts, he gripped me up by my hair and dragged me into the next room, leaving me kicking and screaming, pulling some of my hair out in the process.

"Shut tha' fuck up!" He snapped, slapping me across my face.

I yelped in pain, as he did it again. I tucked my bottom lip, trying to shush my cries, but it was almost impossible.

He grabbed my hands and tied them up against the bedframe. Afterwards, he kneeled and ripped my shirt off. I whimpered, which resulted in another slap to the face. My bottom lip started to bleed and I could feel my face swell up.

Once my shirt was torn off, he unhooked my bra leaving the upper part of my body exposed. His fingers touched my breast, which made me cringe. He chuckled, and licked over his bottom lips, pulling out a pocketknife.

I took a few deep breaths as he dragged it across my stomach. Once he made it past my stomach, he poked it into my chest, running it up.

I hissed as the blade cut my chest slightly. The man stood up and smile, watching the blood drip from my chest.

"Let yo' man know, Richie was hea'." I sat there holding my eyes shut. Why, why was he doing this to us? He already took

Denise away from Troy. I was scared out of my mind and, it was quiet. I opened one eye and he was still standing there.

"Please, what do you want from us? We did nothing to y-you." I cried out. He played with the blade in his hands.

"I want to send a message. Denise looked just like how you are and this knife was the same one I used to slice every inch of her body up with. The little lady put up a good ass fight. The reason why she had a closed casket." He grinned.

"Please, d-don't hurt mme. I won't tell. I…" he cut me off ass he sped up close to me. He ran the sharp knife down my neck again, causing yet another cut. "G-God, please d-don't hurt me." He chuckled.

"This is just a message. Now, go to sleep baby girl." His fist connected with my face and everything went black.

***

"Baby! Wake up. God Marcus help me untie her!" I felt my body being lifted, but I had the most splitting headache and my body ached.

"Who should I call?!" Marcus said frantically.

"C-call, fuck! Call M-Melina, she a nurse. She's the only one I can talk to right now! Go hurry! My baby is bleeding!" The heavy footsteps ran out of the room, but I was still out of it. I was just listening. I couldn't move at all.

"Baby, just move to let me know you and my baby a'ight? Please, Lex." He begged. I groaned and moved my head. Aching in pain, he rubbed my stomach and tried to clean my wounds. As I felt hot tears fall onto my bare flesh.

"I love you. If anything happened I-I don't know what I'd do." I deeply coughed.

"I love you too. H-he sent you a message." I said dry and hoarsely.

"What? B-baby?! What type of message?" He shrieked.

"D-death."

Monet Dragun

Chapter Sixteen
Troy

"Hello, you've reached Melina. Sorry I could." This is the third time I've heard Marcus call Melina and she still didn't answer the phone.

"Fuck is you doing you can't answer the phone!" He yelled. He dialed the number again and had it on speaker phone once again.

"Hello?" Her voice finally said as it came through the phone. I got up and told him to stay by Lex. I grabbed the phone from him and yelled at her.

"At least you can do is answer your damn phone! Yes, this is your son. You need to come to my house right now! I know you're a nurse and Alexus' has been hurt bad! If you had any damn love for me, you'll come over to 5387 Frankly Drive and tell me all the shit you know and help my ba…" she cut me off and rustling was heard over the phone.

"I'm on my way now! Curtis now is not the time for your bull shit! Shut up!" She hung up the phone and I sighed in relief. I looked down at Lex, and she was still out of it. It hurt me to see my baby that way, and that's when reality kicked in.

"Marcus I'm so…" he cut me off and gave me a hug.

"Bruh, you don't have to say it. I didn't want this to happen either, but they den' hit two of our live ones. This has to end before it gets worse." I looked down at Lex one more time.

"But look at her! It has gotten worse. What if he comes after my pops? I can't lose another parent." I said pacing the floor.

"T-Troy?" I looked at Lex and she was really coming to now.

"Baby, you shouldn't be talking, okay? Just take it easy." She began to cry something heavy.

"H-he said, he was going to kill me and Ciara. Just like h-he did y-your mom. He cut her up! Ooh God my baby!" She was in shock and I didn't want her to hurt the baby by having a panic attack.

I knelt next to her and grabbed both of her hands. "Breathe. In and out. Inhale and exhale. In and out." She did as I said as I passed her some water.

"Drink this, your mouth is dry, babe." She did as I told, and she wrapped her hands around my neck.

"I swear, he ain't gone hurt you. I promise you that." She nodded against my skin and I could feel her hot tears making my shirt wet.

"Troy, she's here." I looked up and nodded for him to let her into my room. Me and her needed to talk. And now!

***

"Troy, she's sleep now. She had to get stitches and I had to give her some pain meds. They won't hurt the baby." I nodded as I sat there with my head in my hands.

"Why you leave me?" I finally blurted out.

She sighed deeply and sat next to me. "Because...because I didn't want hhim to hurt you. So, Denise took you in as her son. There wasn't a minute of the day I didn't think about you. Richie wasn't going to leave Denise alone or me, so she took you out of the kindness of her heart." I just sat there soaking everything in that she was telling.

"So, who exactly is Richie?" I probed still not looking at her.

"M-My brother. Him and Denise were married once upon a time, but she refused to have kids with him. So that's where your father came in and swooped her up from his beatings and abuse. He was a good man back then. I don't know what happened. Maybe it was the women or maybe losing Denise, he never loved me like he did her." This is when I was staring at her with a death glare.

"Your brother!" She nodded. "And now what? He's coming for you?" She shook her head no.

"No." I jumped up and she flinched.

"Why?!!" I screamed. And tears trickled down her eyes.

"B-Because he pinned her murder on me. They had no proof though." She said fiddling with her thumbs. I was angry and I couldn't take all the anger that was inside of me. I picked up the beer by lap and smashed it. I began tearing up everything in the house, until Marcus came down the stairs just to hold me back.

"Aye! Troy, chill mane!!" He yelled as he tried to hold me back, but my mouth kept running.

"Melina, this is all your fault! Bitch, my life is fucked up because of you!!" I screamed. She shot up from the couch and slapped me. Her last straw was when I called her out of her name. Even though it was very disrespectful, she deserved it. I had more intense words for her than that.

"Don't you ever call me a bitch!" she yelled, her face growing red. "I'm your mother!"

"Fuck you, bitch! You had the only mother I knew murdered!" I spat at her, breaking away from Marcus.

Melina's face softened as her eyes began to water. I rolled my eyes and laughed at her, balling my fists.

"Cry! I don't give a fuck!" I yelled again. "You weren't fucking crying when you left me or when you let Richie murder my momma! You definitely weren't crying when you got right back wit' Curtis! Was you?"

"It hurt me, Troy! I swear it did! Richie was never supposed to take it that far." She tried to reason with me.

"Richie took it that damn far and he's taking it even further now! He coulda killed both of my babies!" I slammed my fist against the wall, causing her to jump.

"But I saved her life! Shouldn't I get some type of credit for that Troy!?" she cried.

"Credit? You want credit for cleaning up a mess you fucking caused?" I looked at her like she had two heads. "Get the fuck out."

She quickly just gathered her things and left out the house, not saying goodbye. Marcus looked at me and sighed, shaking his head.

"You good bruh?" he asked, patting my shoulder.

I nodded and took a deep breath in. "I think I'm gon' go take a lil' nap wit' Lex and clear my head."

"A'ight, make sure you call me. We got to discuss what we gon' do." he dapped me up and walked out.

I sighed and went up the stairs, sliding into bed next to Lex. She quickly wrapped her body with mine and buried her face in the crook my neck. All I could do was smile and peck her forehead, before closing my eyes and falling asleep as well.

***

Richie

As I sat on my couch and ate some Chexmix, a fews knocks distracted me from my television program. I got up with the bag still in my hands and stretched. The knocking continued but I wasn't about to race to no door.

I finally got to it I opened it and continued to eat my food when I was met with a surprise at the door!

SMACK!

"What the hell! Melina, fuck is wrong with you?! You know I'm crazy!" I yelled wrapping my hand around her throat.

"Fuck off, Richie! What did you do tonight and don't you fucking lie to me!" She said shoving me in the chest.

I smirked and finished eating my food. "Who wants to know?" She slapped me on the back of the head, and I glared at her.

"Don't fucking play coy with me! What did you do? WHAT DID YOU DO!" She said failing her arms at me making me back up off her. The bag fell and the food fell all on the floor.

"I handled bi'ness, again. Who wants to fucking know?" I said calmly.

"You ruined everything! What made you do that girl like that! She didn't do anything. Leave. My. Son. ALONE! You may be my damn brother, but this has gone too far! Leave Troy out of this! I swear if you…"

117

"If WHAT! Remember, I can send your ass to jail! I do have proof. If I fall, you fall too!" I said sitting in my seat and clasping my hands together.

"You're sick! You need help! Don't come near my boy again! I lost him once, I won't lose him again! This time I'll die for mine!" I stared at her and got up.

"You'll do what I tell you, Melina! I swear if you say anything, I don't give a damn if you are my sister, you'll be just like Denise." Her eyes widened and she slapped me again.

"That was once your damn wife and I'm your fucking sister. Don't make me lose my religion in here! Just because you sold your soul to the devil, doesn't mean I will! You will not pin this on me. She was my friend! I made a mistake for sleeping with her husband. You and him had y'all beef! You didn't have to kill her!" I pushed her down and stood over her.

"I killed her for a reason! She knew too much, you knew that!" I screamed. Breathing heavily and hold my hand up I wanted to crack her so bad. Just to shut her up.

"Son of a bitch! Did you know she was pregnant!" She spat leaving me dumbfounded. "She was pregnant by you. She came over that night the night you killed her to tell you, but you found out about her and Curtis and you killed her and that baby! Then you tried to pin it on me because me and her were feuding! This is all your fault! I let you corrupt me, but no more. No more of this! You leave us alone or you'll be the one dead! DON'T COME NEAR ME OR MY SON, NOR CURTIS, or I'll kill you Richie! That's a promise, baby boy." She got up and moved me away from her.

I was in shock. Denise wwas pregnant? If she would have never cheated, she'd still be alive, but like I said, she knew too much. She had to die.

***

Marcus
A Few Days Later...

"How's Lex?" I questioned Troy as we walked into the dark basement.

"She's doing a'ight. She said I was a little wrong for doing Melina like that. What you think?" I nodded.

"Yeah, you called her a bitch and all. Maybe she's trying to fix this with you? You need to let go of your pride and talk to her." He nodded and ran his hand down his face.

"I'ma try, but have you called Ciara to check on her and Lex? They not at yo' crib, right?" He asked.

"Na' they with her moms or somethin' like that. My fam packin'. They ain't gon' run up over there." He nodded and I dapped him up.

"My mans. Now let's finish this nigga off." I nodded and Bucum opened the door for us. Stephen had his head down, breathing uneasily. Blood was everywhere. His white shirt was stained red.

Troy slapped his face waking him up. "Huh, what?! No more, man, n-no more." He stuttered. I laughed and so did Troy.

"Oh, someone's not hard anymore huh?" Troy said leaving in his face. "You ready to die yet?" He questioned.

"You kill me and she's dead! Melina will be dead! Everyone will die! You can't kill me! KING KONG AIN'T got shit on me!" He yelled fear laced all in his throat.

"King Kong ain't got shit on me!" I mocked, causing a few in the room to chuckle.

"That's why I fucked your bitch!" He spat as he spitted blood on my new black timbs.

"Bitch!" I landed all types of punches on his ass, causing his yell out in pain.

"Man, it's time for him to see hell." Troy said darkly. "You want the first pop? Or me?" I grabbed the gun from him and without hesitation I shot him in the chest twice. I handed it to Troy, and he planted it to his temple.

"You were my blood, my damn blood. You talked to a nigga who killed yo' moms! Any last words?" He said as he cocked the gun.

"You won't live the day to see yo' baby! I been ready to die."
Marcus nodded and shot him in the arm, leg, and stomach.
Causing blood to spill out of his mouth.

"I promised you that'll you'll die slow." And with that he
walked out with Stephen gasping for air.

"T-Troy! Y-y-you you f-fucked up-p! H-he gon…"

POW!

"Clean that shit up and make his ass disappear and clean this."
He handed Bucum the gun and he walked out. I didn't think he'd
kill him. I was sadly mistaken.

"Troy, You good?" I asked as walked out of the building.

"I need to go repent my sins." And with that, he walked away
from me with his hands deep in his pockets. I could only imagine
what he was going through or feeling. His life was fucked up, but
I'll be with him to the end, like a brother should.

Monet Dragun

Chapter Seventeen
Troy

They say a man ain't suppose to cry
How can I look my father in the eyes?
How can I sit here on my mother's grave and cry? I killed her son.

How can I cry to God for forgiveness? He was my blood? Right?

All these questions ran through my head as my father got the call that he was missing. Who in the hell reported his dog ass missing?

After what he did? He didn't deserve to be found. I sat there with my head in my hands as I sat on the edge of the bed. I felt Alexus hand on my shoulder.

"Baby, I just need to be alone. When did you get back?" Her hand stayed on my shoulder and I looked up and jumped at the sight before me.

My momma

"Ma'?!" I almost screamed. Her shadowy figure nodded.

"You need to tell him son." I frowned my eyebrows.

"Tell who, what ma'?" I said dumbfounded.

"Tell your father about Stephen. He has the right to bury his son and he has things to tell you." I shook my head.

"Tell me what?! More horrible things? What my father is not really my father? Huh? What more can bring more turmoil on my life ma'! I'm in my twenties and I'm already starting to get grey hairs! What more can possibly go wrong in my life!? Only thing I have is my woman and my friend, that's it!" He arms wrapped around my neck.

"You need peace and he'll bring it to you."

"Who will bring me peace, Denise! Who!" She gave me a weak smile before but her hand on my face and disappeared. I dropped to my knees unable to do anything. I was crumbling. All this would end up putting me in an early grave.

"Troy! Baby, are you okay?" Lex sped to my side and squeezed me. "Why are you on the floor like this?" She questioned as she grabbed my face, trying to get me to look into her eyes, but I wouldn't.

"Talk to me? Are you okay?" I shook my head no.

"I seen her. She told me he would bring me peace." I mumble.

"Who, baby? Who said that?" She said looking around.

"Denise." She sighed and brought me closer to her.

"Baby, everything will be alright. I think you might need some closure babe." I looked up at her as tears threatened to fall. "Baby, it's okay to cry."

"But they say a man ain't suppose to cry and I'm tired of crying, Lex. I did something, I-I think I regret doing it, but he was going to keep hurting us." I sighed.

"What did you do? You can talk to me." I looked her deep in those hazel brown eyes and shook my head at what I just pictured.

"I killed Stephen. I need to talk to my father, and the only closure I'll have is killing Richie." I ran my hands down the scar on her neck and chest and it angered to me that I wasn't there to protect her. This needed to end, and fast. She just stared into my eyes, not able to comprehend what I just told her.

"Baby? That's not going to stop Richie or bring your mama back. Baby, you need to talk to someone."

"Lex, I can't open up to anyone. There's nothing to talk about. I won't be talking to a shrink. This just needs to end."

She kissed my forehead and looked me in the eyes. "Well, Melina is here to talk to you." I should've known this was coming.

"I-I'll go down there and talk to her for you babe, okay?" She nodded and planted a tender kiss on my cheek.

"She needs you and you need her."

***

Marcus

"Ciara? Baby, where you at girl?" I questioned as I trucked up the steps.

"With the baby, shh." She said as she just put her in the bed. "I have to tell you, he's dead babe." Her eyes widened and she closed Sophia's door. "Who's dead? Stephan?" She probed. I nodded and she sighed. A sigh of joy and relief she sighed as if she had a weight lifted off her shoulders. She threw her arms over me and kissed me repeatedly.

"I don't want you to keep anything from me okay? For real baby." She nodded and kept kissing me.

"Since we're keeping it truthful. I must tell you something Lex told me. It's important." I pulled away and looked at her.

"Speak on it, baby."

Monet Dragun

Chapter Eighteen

Marcus

"So? What you got to tell me?" I said to Ciara.

"Well, Alexus said that Richie guy, I think that what his name is, h-he said that if Melina didn't tell Troy the truth," She swallowed hard. "That he'll kill her and him." She said shifting a bit.

"What's the truth, Ciara? What else is Melina hiding?" I said rubbing her back. Trying to get it out of her.

"She said that he said, and I quote "Melina, ain't no angel. She's the one that killed Denise." I don't know if he was trying to sell her out or something but something doesn't sound right about that, right? I don't think Melina would do that. I mean I don't know. I don't know the woman." I was in shock.

"And Lex didn't tell Troy? I see why because Troy is already on the edge." I said rubbing my hands down my face.

"Right. He needs peace really. This isn't right for him or Lex. She's pregnant. She can't be stressed out." I nodded in agreement.

"So, I was thinking. We all need a break from all this bull and need to go some where? What you think about that?" As soon as she was about to respond, Sophia broke out in cries.

"Hold that thought, babe, but I'd love that." She planted a soft kiss on my cheek and made her way to our baby. I sighed and picked up my phone quickly send Troy a text.

Trojan: we need to talk somein' serious. And we all need a break, bruh. Hit me back when you can. One love

***

Troy

As I stopped at the steps, looking at Melina, I sighed and stepped fully off the steps. She rubbed her hands together and I motioned her to have a seat. She nodded and sat down in the chair across from the couch.

"So, first Tr…" I put up my hand for her to stop and I sighed shaking my head.

"You don't have to apologize anymore. I have too. I'm so sorry for calling you…" I coughed and cleared my throat. "I'm sorry for calling you a bitch. That was disrespectful and out of line. I apologize for that." A man must own up to his mistakes.

"I accept, but it was out of anger and I understand, but Troy please understand this. I didn't leave because I didn't want you. I wanted you. I wanted you with ever fiber in my being, Troy. I named you, I birthed you. I couldn't have you because of that damn Richie! I wish he was never my brother. My blood, my own damn blood caused all of this!" I can relate to blood brothers.

"I'm hearing you. Continue." I sighed. She nodded and rubbed her hands down her pants legs.

"Um, Denise, s-she took care of you like her own, and I'm so grateful for that. She helped me when she was the one that needed the help from Richie. He is so, so sick! Troy, I'm sorry for all of this. I wish I could turn back time, but I can't. But you must talk to your father. You must mend things, Troy. You don't want to lose him." I knitted my eyebrows together.

"What do you mean lose him?" I probed.

"Richie. He's a sick son of a bitch! He has some serious beef with Curtis. You need to mend y'all relationship." I shook my head.

"I don't think I can do that. Too much bad blood." I said looking down at my crumpled hands. She grabbed them and made me look at her.

"You need to tell him. You can't have this weighing down on you, son. You need to tell him! He can not judge you. He has his demons too! Let him know, please. If me and you can fix it, so can you and him." She gave me a half smile and I tried to return it. I felt my emotions get the best of me, but I chucked that shit up. "I love you Troy and…"

"If you loved him, then why did Richie tell me you killed Denise?" Lex said coming down the steps and rubbing her tummy. Her pudge is growing and growing, but my head was spinning.

"He is lying! She was my friend, my one and only friend! We all made mistakes!" I looked at her as she had tears in her eyes. "What did he really do to my Denise? Just let me have it. Please." I motioned for Lex to come over to me. She did and hugged me from the back as I rubbed her stomach.

"W-well he called her over. He said he just wanted to fix things and Denise. S-she was a good woman! She didn't deserve what he did to her. When she came over, he cut her up like she was just a piece of meat! He did her like she was animal and I-I came over there to tell him that I wanted nothing to do with him, nothing more! But when I came into that house, I seen her laying there dead and mutilated! Not even knowing what had happened, I ran over to her touching her body, and crying. He came out of the shadows with that same knife and was wiping it clean. She put up a fight though. Indeed, she did." I had a stone-cold look in my face.

"And what did he make you do?" I said my fingers tapping against the couch arm.

"H-he made me put my fingerprints everywhere. I couldn't believe my on brother was going to frame me for murder." She said shaking her head crying. I was furious, but I wasn't about to go through this anymore.

"Thank you for that closure, Melina." I stood up and hugged her tightly. She might be the only thing left that loves me in my life.

"I'ma need to talk to my father and tell him the truth. This needs to be done and dealt with." Melina nodded and she sighed as she walked for the door.

"One day, I hope you can call me mom." She waved and walked out before I could say another word.

"Babe, are you okay?" I nodded and gave her a genuine smile.

"I'ma be fine baby, for real. Things gon' go back to normal. I promise." I bent down and kissed her stomach.

"Troy?" She groaned as I kissed her thick thighs bring the kisses up to her neck.

"Yes?" I said as I gripped her ass a little.

"I want you to off him. You have my full approval." A tear slipped down her eye as she rubbed her scar.

"Baby, shh. You worry about our bun in the oven. He gon' get his. I'ma call for one of my guys to come over here while I go to my pops place. Is that coo'?" She nodded as I swatted her hand away. "You're still so beautiful to me." I said kissing her full plump lips.

"Thank you, babe. Call Bucum over! He makes the best crab cakes." She beamed as she mumbled through my kisses.

"Babe, you can't have seafood though." She gave me a pouty face.

"The hell I can. Me and the baby are cravin' that!" She said as her full accent came out.

"A'ight, a'ight! I'ma call him over. But first," I gripped her ass tighter. "Lemme get some."

Chapter Nineteen
Troy

"Baby, don't you have somewhere to be?" Lex questioned as I kissed over her body.

"Yeah, but…" she cut me off and pushed me up off her, leaving me wide eyed.

"Every time you get get all upset and you're sad, or depressed you want to have sex! No, Troy, no! That does not solve any of your problems okay?" She said with a serious face.

"Baby, it ain't," she cut me off something serious.

"It is like that! I love having sex with you, baby. The reason why I'm glad to be having your first child, but this using sex to fix your problems, is not going to solve a damn thing! You need some help to cope with this. Really baby, I'm only saying this because I love you. Now call Bucum, and go do your bi'ness, and I'm hungry so go!" She said fanning me off and she rubbed her stomach in small circles.

"I don't want to talk to no damn shrink, Lex! So, what if I love your sex, that don't mean a damn thing!" I said starting to get angry.

"It doesn't mean a damn thing? Huh? Really, you're so damn naïve! When you figure it out, you won't be getting none." With that, she stormed up the steps and slammed the door.

"Damn, hormones. Psh! Who is she to cut me off? Me!?" Then I heard her voice.

"Your damn GIRLFRIEND! That's who I am! You're really cut off now!" SLAM! Was the only sound the door made in the house.

I shook my head and grabbed my phone and keys. I cut on the alarm system and called Bucum. On the fifth ring, he answered the phone with a strong hello and a strong cough after.

"You smokin'?" I questioned as I raised an eyebrow.

"Uh, yeah boss, but what do you need?" He questioned.

"For you to not smoke on the job, and for you to come and babysit the wifey." He chuckled.

"Yeah, I'll be over there ASAP boss. One." I nodded as if he could see me.

"One." I hung up and started up my car and pulled out of the driveway, making my way over to my pops house.

"Fuck, this was going to be a long talk." As I pulled off and out of my driveway heading to my dad's house, I wondered how this is going to go?

***

When I got to my dad's house, I got a text from Bucum saying he was with Lex. A sigh of relief came over my body, but if she thought I was going to go see a therapist, she was out her mind. I shook off my thoughts and hopped out my car. I made my way up his path as I stuffed my hand in my pockets.

"Just talk to him. Don't let his ways get to you." I said as I took a deep breath. I knocked on the door and waited for him to open it.

"Hold on!" I heard him say from the other side. I looked down at my feet and huffed. A few seconds passed and the door opened.

"Hey, son. Come on in." He said, his eyes were puffy, and he had a cigarette in his right hand. Oh, God. This was going to be hard.

I nodded and came in. I sat down in the chair as he shut the door and directed his attention to me. "So, what brings you by?" He said putting the cigarette to his lips and taking a puff.

"Well, we've been needing to talk pops, a'ight? I know we ain't been on good terms, but to be honest, we need to get some things straight." He nodded and sipped something dark out of his small glass cup.

"Well, ya' mom..." I put my hand up for him to stop.

"First off, why you ain't tell me Denise wasn't my mama? And Melina is my real moms?! Was that hard for you to tell me?" I questioned.

He laughed and took another sip out of the cup. "Because I didn't know how to tell you and to be honest, I wasn't planing on

Sins of a Thug

telling you. I know we had our differences, but I didn't know how to tell you that. I'm sorry." He shrugged. I squinted my eyes at him.

"You thought? You thought?! Of course, I needed to know that! She wasn't my real mama! But if you would have never cheated on her and my real mom! None of this shit would have never happened period! Plus have some beef with that nigga Richie!" He coughed on the alcoholic beverage and stared at me.

"How do you know about him?!" He yelled slamming the glass down.

"I got connections." He paced the floor and pointed his finger at me.

"You don't know what you're doing! You need to stay out of this and, where's my golden boy? Where's Stephen!" He yelled, out of all of this, he put me through he still believed Stephen was so special to him.

"That nigga dead! Now, how you feel about yo' golden boy! You know, I hate yo' ass? You made my life a living hell. You never loved me!" His eyes glossed and he took a long drag of his cigarette.

"I've always loved you, Troy!" He blew out the smoke. "But what happened to Stephen?! That is my son too." He said in a strained voice.

"He's dead just like I said. I'm sorry pops, but I shot him. He had that nigga Richie, come to my house and hurt Lex an…"

SLAP!

SLAP!

SLAP!

I felt three times across both of my cheeks. I stared at him as my jaw clenched.

"You killed my son! My son! You going to burn in hell, Troy! You were always a bad…" I cut him off. I had enough of this.

"You know my mom came to me and said that you would bring me peace. Now that I know you don't truly love me, I'm done with this father, son shit. Melina will be the one to bring me peace. We're done here. I hope and I pray that God doesn't put

132

you in an early grave. Love thy mother and father, but you've lost
my love. You might want to spread your one and only sons' ashes
across the river, because that's were he is. Bye, Curtis. You don't
have to worry about me, which you never did." I rubbed my
stinging jaw and walked towards the door. I looked at him and
gave him a tight hug. "But just know pop. I forgive you. From
now own, I'm just Troy to you." With that I left out of the house.
A weight was lifted and I'm glad it was.

***

Alexus

"Ciara, but how am I'm supposed to let this go? He is so
uptight, and…" She cut me off and I just rubbed my stomach as
she began to talk rapidly into the phone.

"First, if all, he's been through hell, right?! So, you can't
blame him for wanting to give you that good pipe once in awhile.
Right? Your hormones are everywhere, so you can't just get mad
at him. You love him and he loves you. He just needs you, so keep
being there for him girl. Okay?" I nodded as if she could see me.

"Um, L? Here's your food." Bucum smiled as he poked his
head into my room.

"Awh, thanks! You're the best." He smiled and I motioned for
him to come in.

"Here ya' go. I think boss man gon' be here soon." I nodded
and he gave me a half smile as he walked out. I began to eat, and
damn this was so good. If he wasn't a thug, he could be a damn
good professional chef.

"Hello? Hungry much." Ciara giggled.

"Shush, I…" she cut me off again.

"Hold on, well I'll just call you back. My baby is crying for
me." I laughed.

"Awh, Sophia?" I coped.

"No, girl Marcus." We both busted out laughing and said our
goodbyes. I out my phone down and wiggled my toes as I looked

at the TV. My mind drifted off to Troy. I missed him and my hormonal self did go off on him.

I picked up my phone and scrolled through my phone as I hit his contact. The phone rang and I blew my breath I waited for him to answer.

"Hella?" He said, his accent coming out fully. I could tell he was flustered.

"Baby, when you coming home? Me and jr or princess are missing you." I pouted.

"So You're not mad anymore?" He said. I could clearly tell he was driving.

"Nope. Just come home." My phone buzzed and I pulled it from my ear and looked at my incoming text message.

Stephen: So, how's the baby?

How the hell?! He's dead. I yelled for Bucum and started yelling into the phone. "Baby, hurry up and get home! I got a text from Stephen. He's dead! You said he was dead!" Bucum, ran into my room with his gun.

"Baby, he is! How? Never mind it must be Richie! I'll be there just stay put with Bucum baby. Okay?" I nodded and took a deep breath.

"Okay. Babe, I love you. Just hurry home." I said with all my heart.

"I love you too. I'm almost there. I promise ain't nothing about to happen to you. Never again."

Monet Dragun

Chapter 21
Troy

"Baby? You good? You sure you good? Okay, you're fine. Bucum, I think we're good here. You can go now." I said as I took Lex into my embrace.

"You sure boss? I can just stick here and watch ova' y'all. She's pretty shook up." He said as he scratched his thick beard. I looked down at Lex, and at that very moment, I knew we need security in our house.

"Yeah, you can stay. Plus, she's loves having you here." I cracked a smile and he nodded as he slid his gun in the back of his pants.

"I'll just leave you to alone. I'll be out back." I nodded as I rubbed Lex's back.

"Baby girl? You okay?" I could feel her nod her head against my chest.

"Y-you said he was dead?" She pried.

"He is. Baby I swear it. Lemme see your phone, please." I said softly, as I tried to reassure her and confront her.

"Here." She said as she let me go and grabbed her phone from off the mattress. I grabbed it from her and unlocked it going through the contacts. She had two Stephen's in her phone. One in the contact as my brothers' number, and one with his name under it, but this wasn't from his phone.

It wasn't from him, it had to be from the creep nigga Richie. "How the hell?" Lex came to my side and I ran my hand down my face.

"What?!" She said in a panic tone as she rubbed her belly.

"Richie, got your number how?!" I said in an angry tone. "Get rid of this phone, and we're going to change your number okay? We're going to get some security around hea', okay? I won't have ma' babies in danger!" I yelled, making my full accent to emerge and for Alexus to jump.

"Okay. I'm going to go take a bath." She said softly and turned around.

"Baby, I ain't mean to get loud. I wasn't getting loud with you. I just don't want you to get hurt an..." she stopped me.

"This needs to end! I don't want you in this profession anymore. No more Troy! Please!" She begged as tears ran down her face, but I shook my head no.

"I can't. Until he's dead, I'ma still be in the game. I promise, this will all be over soon." She shook her head.

"No, this is revenge! Do you know what that will do to you Troy? Huh! You're not invincible!" She screamed.

"Baby, don't stress yourself ova' this! Okay? Let ya' man handle this. I never wanted to invoke you in this, but that nigga killed my momma, and hurt you! I'll be damned if I let him live, just so he can hurt more people! No, hell no!" She just stood there as she rubbed her stomach in circles.

"What will happen when our baby is born? Huh, I don't want you into all this when he or she is here. I won't have it!" She was fighting back her tears now. "Either you end this, or you'll lose your family, Troy. I don't want that to happen, okay? Now, lord knows I can't have a drink with this baby in me, but I need some wine!" She huffed.

I scrunched up my face. The hell? She ain't drinking shit with my seed in her.

"You ain't drinking shit! If I see you doing it, I'ma hurt you girl!" She waved me off.

"It's called Google, nigga use it or call my wise mother. Pregnant women can drink wine, you donut." She said with an eye roll.

Donut? Worse comeback ever.

I chuckled at her and say on the bed. She snapped her neck as me as she undid her ponytail.

"And what are you laughing at, Troy?" She questioned.

"I'm laughing at you. Donut? That's all you could come up with?" I laughed again, she just straight faced me.

"Really? What you rather me call you asshole, jackass, burnt lizard, what? Take your pick." She said with a shrug.

"No, cause if you do..." she cut me off.

"You'll fuck me up, blah, blah, blah. Oh, hush. That why your hair looks like some damn burnt noddles. I'm going to pour me some wine and take a bath. Don't disturb me or I'll give you a paper cut on your piney winne. Now, you wanna mess with a pregnant woman? Try me." She stripped out of her clothes and disappeared into the bathroom.

"Damn, hormones." I huffed silently. I didn't want to fuck with her ass tonight.

"Troy!" She called out sweetly.

See, I knew she was crazy.

"What!" I said back in her voice. Causing her to smack her lips.

"Can you get in here with me! After you get my wine and some candles please." I shook my head at how much of a spoiled brat she was, but I lover her ass.

"Yeah, I will. I'll be right back." I heard her reply and I disappeared out if the room and made my way downstairs. My phone started to buzz, and I checked it only to see that Marcus and some others was texting me.

7:45 Monday Marcus: we need to talk somein' serious. And we all need a break, bruh. Hit me back when you can. One love

1 min ago Marcus: I think we need to get out of town for a bit. The girls need a break from all the hell that's been going on. Hit me back, bruh, before I blow yo' shit up and tell Lex. Ya' know she love me.

4:56 Pops: you're my only son na'. I'm sorry. We'll get past this. Love you son.

15 mins ago. Bucum: everythang is looking good, boss.

Just now 860-416-0917: watch ya' back. Ya' never now who's lurkin.

Who this fuck is that and how'd they get my number? But I responded back.

Me: na' homeboy. Watch yours

After I sent the message, I sent Marcus a message telling him we need to do that. I came across my dads' message, but I ain't send him shit.

I walked into the kitchen and grabbed the wine bottle and some glasses. I had to make two trips down here anyway. I trucked up the steps and heard Lex, singing. Singing to our baby.

"Babe? When is your appointment? It's crazy you're four months and not showing yet! You're just so fine with this tiny pudge." I questioned as I walked into the bathroom. I kind of startled her.

"Geez, knock first. You scared me." She said making me laughed. "But, on Thursday, baby." She ran the water up and down her body as she looked up at me.

"Okay, and ugh I'll go see the damn shrink. I promise you, after all this, I'm going to start up football again. Okay?" Her eyes lit up and she pulled me into a short hug and kisses me all over my face.

"Okay, I'm so happy to hear that! I can't wait for you to stop all this and do that. It's what you love." I pecked her lips and the kiss got deeper until I pushed away.

"No sex until I talk to the shrink, okay?" She nodded and rubbed her stomach.

"Okay, I can deal with that. You still cut off though." She smirked.

"Girl bye, woo, dismissed, fuck on! With all that, you my wife and that my pwussy! You can never cut me off, that's mine, but I can cut you off from this dick though. You know you're a freak times a hundred and this dick is what got' ya ass knocked up. Remember, the night you were drunk? That's the night this pipe did ya' too good and got that ass pregnant." She pinched me and smacked her lips.

"Shut up! You're so childish. The reason I got pregnant is because yo' pull out game is weak." She giggled as she splashed some water on me.

"Oh! It's like that?" She nodded and I shook my head. "A'ight, I'll remember that when you're screaming papi chulo! Don't pull out papi! I'm about to..." She cut me off and rolled those beautiful eyes.

"Oh, shut up okay, you win! Now can you go get me some chocolate covered strawberries please!" She pouted.

"Mhm, what I thought." I walked out of the bathroom and made my way to the kitchen. I honestly don't know what I'd do without her. I'd probably be dead or on a way worse path than I am now. I just didn't want to fuss and fight with her about this anymore.

***

Richie

I sat in my snakeskin and leather chair behind my oak desk as I stared at the man sitting in front of me.

"So what brings you to my place of bi'ness?" His eyes squinted at me as I clasped my hands together and stared at him.

"Leave my family alone. You may have taken my wife, but you won't hurt anymore people on my family." I laughed at how serious he was.

"Don't you have a baptizing you need to be doing or giving someone the Holy Ghost? Because back in the day, you my man, wasn't so damn holy." I smirked.

"If you know me, like you say you do, Richie, then you wouldn't mess with me or mine." A grin appeared across my face.

"Is that suppose to scare me? You're a preacher! What are you going to do? God will not forgive you for killing me or your attempt too." I laughed.

"God will forgive anyone for their sins! You? That's hard to believe. He'll reject you at the door!" I fanned him off.

"What are you giggling about? Trying to hurt me and make me feel worthless, huh? Holy water? Nigga you may think you're hard, but you're truly not. You're a bluff and a pussy." I shook my head and picked up my cigar and put it to my lips.

"That's not how Denise felt about me when you were beatin' her and treating her like trash! You wish you had my family. Tou always wanted to be me, but you could never amount to the man I was." I let out the smoke as my face changed in the matter of seconds and so did my anger.

"That was supposed to be my family! Mine! You stole what was mine, so I took what was yours! Why don't you ask my little sister." I smirked. He trained an eyebrow.

"Who's your sister?!" He pried.

"Don't you sleep and fuck her every night, preacher man?" I taunted. He shot up from his seat.

"To hell with you! You're just talkin' horseshit!" He screamed. I laughed again harder this time as I held my stomach.

"Woah! You didn't know? You didn't know she's the very reason why Denise is dead? Man, you're easy pickings because, Denise wasn't to hard to fuck or kill!" He dove over the desk and I didn't see the fury of punches he was throwing until I cracked him once and twice, sending his falling to his feet. He got up like a champ though, and we were going head to head, until I reached for my gun.

"Ya' now. You can fight, but your wife fought better. She was screaming your name and all son. I suggest you love your short life well with the son that should have been mine, because all y'all gone die. You're just lucky I'm letting you live now. "

He didn't flinch. He spat in my face and shoved me away sending one last punch to my jaw.

"You watch your back!" He adjusted his suit and walked to the door. "Because nigga! I'm always packin'!" He said. He opened his jacket and showed his piece. He smirked as I wiggled my jaw and clutched my gun. I had better plans than to shoot him. I'd rather him scream like his little whore of a dead wife. That'll bring me so much fond and happy memories that I could send to his bitch son.

Chapter Twenty
Troy

"Babe, I gotta go to the club and check out somethings. You good by yourself? Bucum is here." she nodded and hugged me and peck my lips.

"When will you be back babe? I wanna cuddle and hold you." She whined.

"Well, I won't be long. Me and Mar got to handle some bi'ness over there, talk 'bout a few things, the usual." She nodded and laid her head on my chest. Moments like this I cherished so much.

"Okay fine, but what's this about us going out of town? I like the sound of that. " she squealed.

"Well, me and Marcus is planning that out. Me and him both know you and and Ciara need a break." She nodded.

"True. So, when is your first therapy session? You know I'm going to, right?" I nodded.

"Fa'sho, I know you got my back, baby girl, but stay off your feet and relax okay?" I kissed the top of her head and she let me go. I scrunched up my face and smacked her ass.

"Uh uh! Where my kiss at guh'?! You betta give me some loving before I go." She smiled and came over to me planted a juicy kiss on my lips.

"There. Now gon', Troy." I shook my head and kissed her belly before I left out of the house. I had more bi'ness to handle than I told Lex. It's somethings she didn't need to hear.

***

As I enter my business, it was quiet, and everyone was getting things set up. As I proceeded to my office upstairs, all my workers nodded and greeted me as I went to my humble office.

When I got up there, I opened the door and this scene was all to familiar. "Marcus, get ya' ass out my seat Cus! Damn, this an everyday thing with you." I chuckled.

He nodded and got up.

"So, have you heard what's been on the streets about Richie?" He sighed and he sat down in the seat in front of me and sunk down in the seat as he held a cigar.

"Nah, what they been saying." He sighed and dumped some of the ashes in the ash tray on my desk.

"That he's trying to take out our bi'ness. This is really starting to get out of hand." I sighed as I rubbed my temples. I inhaled and exhaled trying to figure all of this out.

"We need to get the girls out of this first, then we can handle Richie. I don't want them in anymore danger." He nodded in agreement. "I need a blunt and a drink. Can you call that waitress for me or whatever." I groaned as I rubbed my forehead.

Marcus nodded got up from his seat with the cigar in his mouth as I sat there trying to think of what to do about this situation. It was starting to get way out of control.

"Get yo' ass in hea'! Fuck is you doing here anyway?!" I heard Marcus yell out, which brought my attention from my own thoughts.

"Let go of me! You're fucking up, if you hurt me!" The woman screamed. Her voice sounded vaguely familiar. As I leant up in my seat and waited for Marcus to appear, I could see his figure appear through the foggy glass.

As the door opened, I stood up in anger as he dragged in Ciara's old assistant. "The fuck she doing here!" I yelled.

"Well, this little bitch was faking like she was the damn bartender. I don't know how she got in hea' anyway!" He said as he yanked on her arm.

"How'd you get in hea'?! You were fooling with Stephen, so talk!" Marcus forced her into the chair, and he passed me the blunt. I lit it up and brought it to my lips.

"Speak up! Now!" I demanded. She sat there with her legs crossed and looked in the other direction. I nodded and pulled my spare gun out of the drawer in my desk.

I took it off of safety and cocked it. I know she'll talk now. I pointed it at her, and her head snapped in my direction. Although she didn't do much to me, she did let Stephen into Ciara's office and let him rape her.

"Marcus, you know what to do." He smirked as I tossed the gun towards him. He immediately pushed it against her skull, and she flinched.

"Awh, bitch don't start all that whining shit. You know what you did! Now talk bitch." She but her lip, so he gripped the trigger harder.

"Ya' know. I got a way for making fake tough bitches like you talk." He pointed it at her leg, and she squealed.

"Okay! Okay! Please, okay. I'll talk." She screamed as she put her hands up in defense.

"Exactly. Now, tell us what we need to now, doll." He said with a smile on his face as if I.

She sighed. "Well, I really didn't know he raped her and…" he pressed the gun harder against her thigh.

"Lie again, bitch." She nodded.

"He told me, and she later, fired me. So, I was mad. Richie made a deal with Stephen or something like that, and he had paid me to work here and keep an eye on you two." She shook as she spilled out everything.

"So, if I shot you, you're worth something, huh? And how exactly do you know Riche? You didn't say Stephen introduced y'all or somein' of that nature." She nodded.

"That's because, I-I really think. You don't want to shoot me. Richie is my father." Me and his jaws dropped.

"Oh! You cannot be damn serious! You can't?!" I yelled as I planted both of my hands in my desk and blew out smoke.

"Don't worry, your Denise is not my momma nor Melina. Okay?" On the inside, I let out a breath of relief. "He had me way before he met your mommas." She stated.

"So, you know every little thing huh? So how can we trust you?" Marcus said thinking exactly what I was.

"I know my pops is crazy, but if you kill me, you all will literally be killed in a matter of days. I thought that I had escaped my crazy dad's life, but I was pulled right back into it!" She yelped. I don't know if she was telling the truth or if she was lying.

We needed to use her to our advantage. "Let's just say, you try anything bitch, snd I'll kill yo' ass in a heartbeat! You got that!" She slightly nodded. "I wanna hear a yes or no!" I yelled as I blew smoke into her face.

"Yes. Yes, I understand." I nodded and sat in my seat.

"Good, wanna drink? Because you're going to tell me everything. Every last detail you now about Richie and what he's up to now." She sighed and began to talk.

This was going to be a longer day than I expected.

*****

Richie

As I laid in my bed, with some broad next to me, I heard the doorbell being ring. I groaned and slipped on some boxers as I got out of the bed.

I trucked down the long stairs and proceeded to the door. "Stop ringing my damn doorbell!" I yelled as I went to open the door and was met with my little sister Melina.

"Melina, what you want?" I groaned as she stood at my doorstep.

"For you to leave my family alone! Please." She begged. I shook my head.

"It's a price he had to pay and he ain't pay it. So..." she cut me off.

"You can't hold this grudge forever! Please." I shook my head at how desperate she was.

"What are you going to do for me? Huh? Just say it. You know what to say." I smiled as I clasped my hands together.

"I-I'll confess about what actually happened to Denise that night. " she cried.

"Good girl, you have my word. Shake on it?" I raised an eyebrow.

"Why do I feel like making a deal with the devil?" She whined as she hesitantly pushed her hand towards mine.

"Little sis, you should know I worse than the devil." I smirked. Little tears cascaded down her eyes as she shook my hand. "Okay, now get out. I won't mess with your little family anymore. Just keep your end of the bargain, kay?" She nodded and I smiled to myself. "Now, goodbye." I pushed her out of my house and locked the door. Turning my alarm system back on, I went back up to my room, where this little broad was laid up in this bed still.

A little sex before I continuinf my plan won't hurt none. Melina had no idea what was in store for her and her little family.

Monet Dragun

Chapter Twenty-One
Lex

Sitting on the couch with the teddy bear, Troy bought for me months ago. I was occupied with watching the new TV series on BET called *Sisters* by Tyler Perry.

After, about 50,000 repeats of the commercial, I decided to watch it. Bucum came from checking the house, so I decided to talk to him.

"Hey, Buc!" I said with a smile.

"Hey, sweetheart. What ya' up too?" He questioned. I patted next to me for him to have a seat. He nodded and did so.

"Nothing just watching TV. Bucum?" I said calling his name, as I bit the skin off my bottom lip.

"Yes, Lexy?" He was the only one that called me that.

"Well. I want you to promise me something." I said with a small deep breath.

He nodded once again. "Sure anything?" I fiddled with the ear in the teddy bear before I spoke.

"I want you to make sure Troy is okay. Alright? I just have this feeling. I don't like it either. I just know something bad is going to happen. I just want you to promise me that nothing bad will happen to him." He grabbed my hand and have me a small smile.

"Lexy, nothing bad will happen to him. I promise you that okay? Don't worry you pretty little self over that, okay?" He said as he pulled me into a side hug.

"Fine." I still had this horrible feeling. I just needed to hear his voice. I excused myself and got up to go into my room.

I pulled out my phone and pressed his contact.

"Sup, lil mama." His voice made me feel a little bit at ease.

"Hey, where you at?" I asked. He sounded busy in the background and of course I could hear Marcus.

"At work. Was'sup baby? You a'ight?" He probed.

"I'm fine, love. I just needed to hear that sexy accent of yours." He was quiet for a moment.

"Lex? What's really wrong? Tell me." I sighed and sat halfway on the bed.

"It just I have this horrible feeling that something bad is going to happen..." he cut me off.

"Hol' up real fast, babe. Stay on the phone." I hummed an okay and tapped my index finger on my phone as I played with the ends of my hair.

I then heard his voice and Marcus' deep voice at the same time.

"What the hell? You know who you fucking with?! Get the hell out my place." My heartbeat started to pick up.

"Troy?!" He couldn't hear me. The multiple loud voices drowned out my small timid voice.

"That trick set us up!"

Pow! Pow!

Oh, God what was happening!

"Bitch, you shot me! Fuck what she said kill that bitch ass nigga!"

"Marcus get down!!!" I heard through the phone.

"TROY!" I screamed. Holding my chest, Bucum busted into my room as I held the phone to my ear listening to every last detail.

"They shot, Troy!!! Oh, God man, Get up!!! Code red! Code red! Get them niggas!" Shots rang out and I wouldn't let these tears fall.

I had to be strong for him and for our baby.

"Who sent then bluff ass niggas!" I could hear Marcus shout. "Damn, they clipped me too. Shit hurt like a bitch. Is that bitch dead?" I could hear him yell.

I could hear clicks and okays.

"Who! Aw, nah' Richie sent em'?! Troy don't you do this shit to me and stay awake! Stay up! You gotta stay up for Lex and ya' baby man! Stay awake!!"

Don't cry, Lex! Don't you dare shed a tear.

"Awh, fuck! Man, he's bleeding bad! Where's his phone! Shit, find it!!!" He yelled to someone in their group.

I couldn't speak, I could utter a word.

"FUCK! Lex was on the phone. Hello, baby girl?! Are you still there!!"

"Lexy, hand me the phone." I was frozen. "Lexy!" Bucum shouted, snapping me out of my state of shock.

"Marcus!! W-what is he... oh my God!!!" I cried out, feeling those salty ass tears come. I wouldn't let them fall. I had to be strong. He wasn't leaving me. Je said he'd never leave me!

"Baby girl, give the phone to Bucum, and go sit down. Everything's fine. He's okay." He was lying to spare my feelings and my baby.

I just handed the phone to Bucum and stood there holding myself. This could not be happening. It couldn't be!

I had to sit down before I feel out. I rubbed my stomach, silently pray.

"We have to go to the hospital, Lexy." I shook my head no.

"I can't see him like that! I can't! I have to be strong. I'm his rider." He pulled me up into a hug.

"You are. You need to come with me. It's okay to cry." I shook my head no fighting these damn tears.

"It is not okay! It's not okay! I knew this would happen! Why didn't he listen to me! Why!!!" And now, the tears finally flowed.

"Come on baby girl. You know he ain't going nowhere. Don't say that." I shook as I cried out loud.

"I can't do this." He pecked the top of my head.

"Yes, you can. You're the strongest woman I ever met. And Troy ain't going no damn where. We all know that." He said. In my heart I did too.

The phone call ended but the music continued to play from the other room, the lyrics played out my reality. That just made the tears come faster and harder. That's all I could hear, I couldn't hear Bucum telling me to come on. I could just feel his arms around me as he led me out of the room.

"Keep it on the down low
I don't belong to you
Ain't no white house, ain't no picket fence

Baby you know we don't want the same things
While you're caught up in your feelings
I feel the same as I did yesterday
Baby we've been through this and I feel the same way
I know you don't wanna hear this, and I hate to say it, babe
I done told you, I done showed you
Now you wanna act like I tricked you
But I'm sleep, can't you see?
There's a difference between me, you and these sheets"

Chapter Twenty-Two
Marcus

"C'mon! You my boy you gotta wake up. Don't let that slum ass nigga take you from your girl and unborn baby yo'. " I looked at him as he laid on in the hospital bed.

"Um, sir we need to take care of your wound." The nurse mumbled.

"I'll be fine! I need to know if my friend is going to be okay!" I shouted.

"Sir, please come over here and lower your voice." She said trying to get me to leave out of the room.

"No! My potna' needs me. I'ma stay my black ass righ' hea'." I said snatching away from her.

"Um, are you gay?" I scrunched up my face at her.

"Bitch, I'm trying to be real damn nice but yo' ass is pushing it!" I said in my Chris Tucker voice.

"Sir, you're going to have to leave this room now." I smacked my lips and walked past her. She was still trying to tend to my arm, but I put my hand in her face.

"It's a graze wound. Damn, it'll heal. Fuck out my face. Talkin' bout some am I gay? Bitch, is you gay? With all that glossy ass shit on yo' lips looking like you been smacking on some damn chicken. Got me fucked all the way up. My friend in there half dead and you talking bout' some am I gay?" She bit her lip and turned on her heels walking away.

I shook my head and wondered where Alexus was.

"Baby!" I looked up and looked around. I know I just heard, CiCi voice.

"Marcus!" I looked down the left hallway and seen Ciara speed walking with Phia in her carrier.

"I'm glad you're here." I said as she ran into my arms.

"Of course! I got here as you told me! Are you okay? How is he? God you're bleeding!" She said in a frantic tone.

"I'm good, baby. Chill. But Troy." I kind of trailed off on that part.

"What about him?" I heard Lex yell as she walked quickly towards us. I gave her a hug, avoiding her belly in the process.

"Is he okay?! Please tell me he is!" She screamed as she looked in the glass window.

"I don't know. The nurse kicked me out. They won't tell me nun'. Shit! That was not supposed to go down like that." I said sliding down the wall.

"CiCi, you want me to take the baby to the baby center downstairs?" She nodded at Bucum and passed him to her.

"Nah' I wanna hold my baby. After what happened tonight, I need to hold her." Bucum nodded and passed her to me. Her soft little face brought a little bit of hope into my heart.

"Everyone to room, 305 stat! He's convulsing, code nine! Code nine!" The white nurse yelled as she screamed into the intercom.

I looked up at Troy's room. Room 305. I shook my head back and forth and put Sophia in Ciara's arms.

"What's happening to him?" Lex screamed trying to get one of the nurses or doctors to tell her something, anything.

"Ma'am, we are trying to get him stabilized please, stay out here!" She said slipping into the room. She looked into the glass window with tears in her eyes.

The nurse closed the bluegray curtains, shutting her out of everything. "No! No, Troy!" She screamed as she tried to run into the hospital room, but they pushed her out. Ciara came by her side and held her.

She was holding her by her side. I felt like there was nothing I could do but, sit there and fucking wait!

"Why, him! Why! Lord, please don't take him from me. He's all I got." She cried.

All I could think of is all the bullets that went into his chest. They were trying to kill him. None of us were prepared for that. None of us. Richie's so-called daughter got shot in the process of it all.

Sins of a Thug

I don't believe that was his daughter at all. I believe she was a plant in the beginning. I just wish all of this could have turned out differently.

***

Hours went by and were in are same positions. Sophia was asleep in her carrier and I just hoped and prayed that Troy could see his baby.

"Did you call his parents?" I questioned Lex. She just nodded as she laid her head in Ciara's lap. Ciara ran her hand on Lex's head. You could hear Alexus soft cries.

"You gon' have to relax okay? For that baby growing inside of you. A'ight? " she nodded and I kissed her forehead.

"Alexus! Where's my son! Where's our son!" We heard a man, which would be Troy's father yell as he came jogging down the hall with Melina by his side.

So odd, he never was so loving.

"Where's my baby!" Melina had tears in her eyes. I couldn't believe this.

"He's in the operating room." I mumbled.

"God, please watch over my son." He prayed. I looked up at him and got up. I could feel Ciara grab me, but I pulled away.

"God? You call yourself a preacher? Now he's your son! Now you wanna love him since he's in here! He wouldn't be here if it wasn't for you two!" I screamed.

"Sir, please keep your voice down." The nurse said to me, as she stood up from her desk. I just shook my head and leaned against the wall.

"I made some mistakes! Okay, but Marcus don't throw it in my face. I love my son, no matter what! I didn't want this, none of this!" I scoffed and laughed in his face.

"Funny way of showing it." A white man walked up to us and took his glasses off.

"Family of Griffin, Troy?" He asked as he looked at his clip board.

"Yes, is he going to be alright?!" Lex said with glossy eyes. He sighed and looked more at the papers.

"Ma'am, the bullets hit some vital organs. His jaw is wired shut and he's going to be on a crutch for a while. He's lucky to be alive right now. I see he has a lot to live for." He said pointing at Lex's stomach. She clutched her chest taking a deep breath.

"Well, can I see him?" He shook his head no.

"Not at this moment. I'm sorry. We don't know how stable he is right now, but we'll keep you posted. He's heavily sedated right now. We don't want him to slip." She looked down and nodded.

"You sure he's going to be okay?" He sighed once more.

"He's a trooper, but it's all on him now. If he slips, he may need a transplant. Now we're just playing the waiting game." I could hear Lex crying again.

"Okay, thanks doc." He nodded.

"You all need to pray. Troy needs it right now." And with that he walked away.

"I want us all to hold hands." Melina said speaking up. "Right now." We did as she said. I gripped Lex's hand tight, trying to be strong for her.

"Bow your heads and close your eyes." We all did, even a tear slipped down my eye.

"Oh, Heavenly Father. We come to you for your humble graces, to bring Curtis and I's son back to us. Lord, please guide him back to us for Alexus and their unborn baby. Please, Lord it is not his time yet. Have his mother Denise bring his heavenly wisdom and not let the devil stir him of course. Bring him back to us Lord. In the name we pray, Amen." She spoke beautifully.

"And Lord, tell Troy and Denise I love them. Amen." Curtis added in we all looked up and he had heavy tears in his eyes.

"I'm sorry. Excuse me. He held his hand over his mouth," and he excused himself.

Melina followed after him. Ciara held onto Lex, as they cried. I picked up my sleeping baby and rocked her softly in my arms.

"You gotta wake up man. Your goddaughter and unborn child' need you. We all do."

"I need my son, Melina. I should have not treated him like that. God knows I love that boy. I wish Richie would go to hell. I know he did this. I know it." I could hear Curtis say.

"You know what I have to do. This was his warning I must tell the police I killed Denise to take it off of him. I'll do this to save my son." She cried.

"Damn, Stephen for making this even worse for us. Damn him!" He whispered.

"Did you tell him?" She pried. "Please tell me you tol' him that ain't his brother or your son?" He shook his head.

Stephen wasn't his brother?!

"Nah I couldn't hurt him no mo' then I already have. I'ma failure, Melina. I failed Troy and Denise. I even failed God. Now my son his laying in there half dead. It should be me!" She grabbed his face.

"Don't say that. This will all be over soon. It will." He shook his head.

"How! You tell the police and he's still going to terrorize us. I love you. I'm not letting you go." He held her closer to him.

"CiCi. Go to the car and take Lex and the baby. Y'all need some rest." She nodded and she did what I said. I took a deep breath and went over to Troy's parents.

"I know how to solve this. We gotta off Richie." They both looked at me with shocked faces.

"Did you ..." I cut him off.

"Me. G, I heard everything and Melina you can't leave your son. This gotta' be done for Troy." It took them a minute, but they nodded.

"For Troy."

Monet Dragun

Chapter Twenty-Three
Marcus

I was laying on the brown couch with Sophia on my chest. Yes, I was still in the hospital. Ciara had come this morning and brought my baby with her again.

"Mar? You need some rest. Are you hungry?" I shook my head no. "You have to eat. I know your bestfriend is fighting for his life, but you need to eat. Okay?" I sighed.

"How is Lex? I questioned, getting her to get off me. She sighed and sat in the seat across from me.

"She's doing fine. She's at the crib with her mama. She needed to stay off her feet." I nodded and rubbed Sophia's back.

"How is he?" Melina said as she stirred in her sleep. I shrugged.

"We don't know yet." I said rubbing my eyes.

"Did you get any sleep?" Ciara asked as she kissed my forehead. I sighed.

"Baby, you already know the answer." She nodded and grabbed Phia.

"She needs to be changed, and she's starting to get cranky." I nodded and sat up dusting my head off.

I looked over at Melina and she had tears in her eyes. I got up and sat next to her.

"Everything will be okay. You know that man is strong. He's going to make it. You gotta have faith in your son." She nodded.

"I've always had faith in him." She smiled. I looked at her and I had to ask this question.

"Why did you give him to Denise?" She sighed and wiped her tears.

"Truthfully? It was all because of my brother and how he had already ruined so many lives. Troy was always supposed to be hers. If I would not have slept with her husband, we wouldn't be in this mess. I didn't want him to be hurt by my own brother, so I did it to save him. The fact that Denise got caught up in this bullshit and got killed over my selfish decisions. I loved him, nonetheless and I always will." She gave me a small smile and I rubbed her back.

"Where is Curtis?" I probed. She looked around and shrugged.

"He was just here a moment ago. Maybe he's in the with Troy." I frowned my eyebrows.

"We can't go in yet." I stood up and I went around the corner to see him with his head pressed against the glass window, crying. I sighed and motioned for Melina to go over to him.

He shouldn't have done his son like that. Now he is crying over how he did him. It was kind of to late for all that. He can be gone, and he'll be stuck with what he did to him.

Bucum walked over to me and handed me his phone. "You need to hear this." I grabbed the phone and listened to the message.

"Is he crazy?!" I said to him he nodded agreeing with me.

"This gotta end before something else goes wrong." I nodded and closed off the phone. I don't know what else can go wrong.

I wanted to chuck this damn phone across the room. Richie was crazier than I thought.

The same white doctor from last night came up to me. "You guys can see him now. His surgery went well. He's just sleeping right now." I nodded and Ciara sat next to me with Phia knocked out in her arms.

"Well we can see him now. Can you call Lex and tell her she can come to the hospital? I know she wants to see him." She nodded and pulled out her phone as she rocked Phia. I went over to Troy's parents and I told then they can go in. Seeing my boy like that was hard, tubes every which way.

He looked pale and just out of it. I just knew if Melina couldn't take that, then neither could Alexus.

I went to his side and grabbed his hand. "Bro, if you can hear me. We gon' get that nigga." Surprisingly he gripped my hand and his eyes slowly parted.

"We..." I cut him off, I knew he didn't even have the strength to talk.

"Bruh, save your strength." He gripped my hand again.

"I w-want him dead, a-and I want'a k-kill him." He said dryly. He closed his eyes, taking a slow breath. His jaw was wired shut, so it was hard for him to even get those words out.

"Baby, don't you talk okay. Just get you rest." A tear slipped down his eye.

"I-I love you, M-Mama. I-I-I'm sorryy." He barley managed to get out. Tears slipped down her eyes as she kissed his for head.

"No need to be sorry baby." Curtis tried to hold in his cries.

"Son, I hope you'll forgive me. I'm so sorry for how I treated you. I'm so sorry." Troy nodded and mumbled an 'I love you too.'

On everything it was time for Richie to go down.

My phone buzzed and I took it out walking to towards the door.

I looked at it, and the message had his location and all. His time was coming soon.

***

Troy

I laid there staring at the ceiling. I could hardly move. Everything was sore as fuck.

My eyes were watery as I heard the door open. My eyes shifted and there stood Lex. I wanted to smile but I couldn't.

"Baby, I hate that you have to lay up like this. Just know me and the baby are fine." I found the strength to nod.

She laid on the side of me and I wanted to hug her so bad. I couldn't even talk to her. Her hand ran down my face and she kissed me.

"Just know I'm going to take care of you. I got'chu. " I could feel her smile against my face. She was being strong for me and I was grateful for her.

"I-I-I'm going to do f-f-football. I-I c-can't do this n-no more. I-I thought I-I was going t-to die." Tears filled my eyes and she wiped them away.

"No, you weren't. You were going to come back. Your momma helped you, didn't she?" I found the strength to nod.

"That's all that matters. Me and the baby love you Troy. My Trojan solider."

"I love–" she shh'ed me.

"You don't have to say it. I know you love us too. Get some rest."

And I did just that. I was going to kill Richie as soon as I got out of this hospital bed. He was going to be the one with the bullet in his face. I placed the AirPods in my ears and began listening to Pop Smoke's 'Got It On Me'. And every rap he spat was my life.

"Have mercy on me, have mercy on my soul
Don't let my heart turn cold
Have mercy on many men
Many, many, many, many men
Wish death 'pon me
Yeah, I don't cry no mo'
I don't look to the sky no mo'"

If niggas thought, they could ice me out they had a another thing coming and that was going to be a bullet straight to the chest. I never wanted my life to go this route, neve in my mind would I have pictured myself laying in a hospital bed. But God knows I'm thankful, even with all my sins, thus had to be the last one. It had to be for the sake of my girl and child on the way.

Chapter Twenty-Four
Troy

I sat up in the bed as Lex tried to feed me some food, but I wasn't goin'.

"Troy, you got eat this now. Come on so I can get the straw in your mouth right." I frowned and crossed my arms over my chest.

"T-this sh-shit g-gross." I managed to mumble out. She sighed and put the mushed-up drink down.

"But babe, you gotta eat. You can't move your mouth, so you have to deal with what you have. You can't go hungry because you're hard Troy. Now eat this food." She said more sternly.

"N-nah." She gave me a look and sat the drink down.

"Stop being a hard ass and drink this damn food! I am not playing with you. You're acting like a child now." I rolled my eyes and looked at her.

"F-fine. D-don't c-curse at t-the c-crippled m-m-man." She shook her head. She looked so frustrated. I rubbed her hand with my almost good one and looked her in the eyes.

"I'm okay. Stop looking at me like that. Now, open your mouth a little if you can." I continued to look at her as I opened my mouth as much as I could.

Pain shot through my jaw and I cringed a little. I hated being helpless/ I hated being in this damn bed. I hated all of this.

"Stop looking at me like that, Troy. Damn." She mumbled. She pulled the straw fork my mouth and damn that stuff was gross.

"W-why? Y-you're b-beautiful." She half smiled and kissed · my forehead softly, but she seen the pain on my face.

"Baby you don't need to talk, okay? You're going to have to type it out or write it. You look like you're in so much pain." I shook my head as she leaned her head on my shoulder. I rubbed my stomach and she giggled.

"That stuff can't be that bad, Troy." I gave her a look and she laughed. She picked up the drink and sipped it through the straw instantly making a gagging noise.

"What in God's name is this!" She said putting her hand on her mouth and sitting it down. "You are not eating that." She mumbled. I just gave her another look as she turned around to look at me. She sighed. "I'm sorry. I should have known you weren't being a baby about that food.

"Sh-shit t-that." I groaned and snatched the pen and paper from my lap. She seen the anger on my face and she just looked at me.

I began to write and passed it to her.

"That shit tasted like shit! Ima see they non cooking asses!" When she looked at me, she had tear dots in her eyes and my face softened.

"I hate that you even have to go through this. Look at you baby. This pains me to see you so hurt." She wiped her eyes and my left thumb rubbed against her cheek. She grabbed my hand and small smiled.

I wrote some more on the paper and passed it to her.

"Baby, you're so strong and I love you for that. We won't be going through this for long." She looked at me and she opened her mouth to speak.

But Marcus stepped in. "Um, Lexy you mind if I speak to him?" She nodded and kissed me softly. She got up and patted him on the chest as she waddled out of the room.

I nodded at him and he say across from me.

"Bro. It's some things you gotta' know and ya' people taking to long to tell you." I cocked my head to the side. And wrote something down for him to head.

"Go on." He nodded.

"Okay, sorry to drop the bomb on you, but Stephen's snake ass wasn't your brother. Real talk, don't blame yo' father even more than you already have. He been out there an emotional wreck. He did this to save yo' life. This man is ready to go to war for you. Melina been out there trying to talk him out of seeing Richie. Yo' old man got heart real talk. I know you heard the things he said to you when you were, you know." I nodded briefly.

I knew Stephen was off. I just knew it, but for my father to keep it from me was wrong if him, but I couldn't hold it against him any longer.

I wrote something down again for him. I was getting tried if this shit right hea.

"I'm glad he wasn't my bro. Real shit, but I want y'all to stake out Richie's place. Find out everyone he knows, everyone! That little bitch of a daughter he so-called got? I want her dead also. I'm taking down his whole empire, and when I get back on my feet, even if I still gotta messed up leg, Ima kill his ass myself."

I passed it to him, and he looked up at me before he read. He scanned the paper and sighed.

"You need to worry bout..." I put my good hand up for him to stop.

"E-either y-you by m-my side or y-y-you against m-me, Bruh." I held out my fist and he dabbed up my fist.

"You know I'm with'cha brother. Till the day we die." I nodded and looked out the window.

I wanted out of this damn hospital. I wanted that niggas head.

***

Lex

I was with my momma at me and Troy's house, trying to get everything ready for him.

"Momma, I'm so worried about him. Knowing him I know when he gets home, he is going to bent on getting his enemy. Knowing that he has a wired jaw, he does not care. He is just too strong, and he can't back down from anything." She nodded as she out some of his clothes into a a duffle bag.

"Baby, he is a strong man. We all know that and what he's been through. Maybe he does need this to let it all go. The man killed his momma, well the woman who raised him. He just needs that closure." I nodded totally agreeing with my mom.

"You think after all this he'll quit this game? I want him to do what he loves. Football. He has no one to stop him now." I sighed.

"Only he can stop himself, Lex. You know that." I nodded and shrugged my momma.

"I love you." I sniffed.

"Girl, you and these hormones." I laughed and was about to say some before someone knocked on the door loudly.

"You stay right hea', I'll go get it." I nodded. My momma was always strapped. She ain't play them games.

I heard the door open and close. "Lex!" I got up rubbing my stomach as I went down the steps.

"What is it momma?!" She held this box and opened it.

"The hell is that?!" We both screeched.

"A dead ass rat." He said lowly.

"What do you think this means?!" I said holding my nose.

"All rats die. Call Bucum and Marcus. We don't need Troy stressed, okay? Go righ' now, we have to leave."

I did exactly what my momma said. I can't believe I still wasn't safe I my own damn home. This has got to stop. We can't live like this. My baby can't live like this. I grabbed my phone and hurriedly called Mar and B.

I had to be calm about this.

Chapter Twenty-Five
Troy

Sitting in the hospital bed was horrid. I couldn't move like I wanted too. I couldn't do shit put sit here and look pitiful.

There wasn't a damn thing on TV and I just wanted to get up and leave and be with my two babies.

There was a slight knock on my door. I didn't understand why they knocked like I could talk.

I just rolled my eyes and mumbled loud enough for whoever to hear me and come in.

And, sure enough. It was my pops.

"Eh, hey son." He said as he rubbed the back of his head.

"Sup– f-fuck!" I groaned slamming my head back causing slight pain in my jaw.

"I'm sorry this had to happen. I really am. I'm sorry for doing you the way I did. I'm such a fuckup!" I looked at him with wide eyes. I heard him curse, but they were in the bible. "Forgive me Lord." He made a cross over his heart and chest and kissed his hands up to God. "Again, I'm sorry and I owe you so much. I'm paying you every cent back that Stephen took from you. I'm sorry for not tell you he wasn't your brother, but I could say anything. This is all Richie. I swear to you that." I nodded and pulled out a fresh piece of paper.

"So is Stephen related to Richie of some sort?" I wrote down and passed it to him. It was all out of curiosity and I wouldn't be angry if he was.

I've been through lie after lie so, this wouldn't be new.

"In the biblical no. He was adopted." I wrote something down.

"Adopted from hell? Maybe." I held it out and he grabbed it. He gave me a serious look and I shrugged.

"I was supposed to make your life a living hell and I can't believe I let him cause me to do that to you. I drove your mother mad. I wish, I wish I would have killed him before I got saved! This is all my fault. I loved her. I loved her to death. I wish I could hold her sometimes. Kiss her, and such. If I would have never cheated, none of this would have went down the way it did. I broke Denise's heart and I hurt Melina's way too many times. I lost one woman, and I'm almost of the bridge of losing another." He inhaled as all the tears flowed.

I never seen my dad cry, ever. And I mean that shit, that man has done some shit. And now he wants to cry. I broke my barrier of hatred if him and raised my hand to rub my old man's shoulder. This is almost the closest we've ever been.

"I really loved Denise. I was just a dog. I don't know why Melina is even with me now."

I grabbed the pen and paper and began to write.

"Maybe she saw that you deserved a second, or forth chance. Maybe she loves you like you love her." I passed him the paper and he scanned over it sighing.

"I do not deserve another chance from your mom. I never did. I don't love your mom like she loves me, and she knows this. I could never replace Denise. I could never find another woman like her." The door creaked and there stood my mom. She had tears in her eyes, but she didn't say anything.

She just stood there clenching her handbag. she looked so hurt broken. "M? How long have you been standing there?" He said looking down at his feet.

"T-the whole time. I'm sorry Troy. I need to do what needs to be done. I love you son." She stood there with this look, and I knew this look.

She held onto that purse and darted out of my room. "Mom!" I called after her. My jaw was sore like the gates of hell.

I couldn't let my mom, my birth mom, go like this. She was going to go kill Richie in cold blood. I knew that look. I had that look one to many times.

I grabbed my casted leg and hobble towards the door clutching the wall for support.

"Son! You can't walk!" He said trying to grab me.

"Let me be! I-I have to g-go get her! M-mom!" I shouted as I was inches from my door and seen her running down the hall in the tiny heels.

"I'll tell Marcus and Bucum. You need to lay down. You can't do anything." Tears ran down my eyes.

"G-g-go g-get her, dad. P-please." I looked at him with pleaded eyes and he looked away. "What kind of man are you!" I pushed him aside and walked out of the room.

Marcus almost ran into me. Trying to catch his breath. "Richie! We gotta get this nigga. He sent this to y'all house man." He showed me a pic on his phone of a dead rat. I punched the wall with my hand that hand a cast on it do I didn't feel a thing.

"Chill, Fam! Yo' girl and her momma in safe hands. We need to make a move Troy. What's it gon' be man? You gotta tell me now." I tried to breathe slowly but it wasn't working.

I grabbed his phone back and typed something for him to read.

"Go find my mama and stop her from tryna kill Richie's bitch ass. I can't have my mama go down 4 her brother's bs! When I get my strength up, I'ma kill his ass on sight. Jus protect my family." I passed him his phone and he read over it.

"You sure about this?" He said with a worried look.

"T-this sh-shit p-personal. I'm d-damn s-sure about t-this." I hobbled back to my room and slammed my door. My dad stood there looking out the window and all I could do was shake my head.

"S-some man y-you are."

Monet Dragun

Chapter Twenty-Six
Troy

I stared at myself in that bathroom mirror. Things were going to change after this. I stared at the stitches in my face and I was never going to be like this again.

I turned away from that mirror and and pushed out of that bathroom on these damn crutches. I limped over to my bed and sat down. I grabbed my phone and quickly called Marcus. He picked up in the third ring. I rubbed my blond curls and adjusted my leg.

"Was'sup? Bro, you good?" I sighed.

"Bruh, I'm good is my girl and her mama okay?" I questioned.

"Yup, I ain't gon' say where they at righ' now though over the phone." I nodded as if he could see me.

"Okay, now that we got that out the way. It's going down tonight. Come pick me up from this damn hospital and no questions. This shit ending tonight. I'ma find out where my momma at." I stood up and I balanced on my good leg. I spoke as well as I could with this damn brace in my mouth.

"Okay bet. I been waiting on ya' call man." I pulled on my shirt.

"T-That's why-y we fam. A'ight one." He said it back and I hung up. My dad came into my room and looked at me.

"What?" I asked as I tossed my iPhone on the bed.

"What are you doing? You can't..." I cut him off with a crazed laugh.

"Are you serious? I'm doing what a real man is supposed to do! Protect and fight for his family. I'm gone." He was about to open his mouth to speak but he didn't even try it.

I moved my crutches and tested how good I could walk on my leg. I was gon' strive through all this pain to get rid of his ass. This all was going to end, and tonight was the night for it.

I pulled on my jacket that Lex had brought over here for me. All I could think about was her safety and wellbeing. I was not

170

going to let anything happen to her. If it did, I don't know what I'd do with myself.

My dad just left out of the room. I didn't give a damn if he didn't care. I was going to end what he was supposed to do a long time ago.

"I just want to let you know that your mama didn't come home last night." I stop what I was doing and looked at him.

"W-what do you mean?" He sighed and ran his hand down his face.

"I don't know. I guess she just didn't want to be bothered with me. She may be at her house, but I have a real strange feeling. I can't even shake the way I'm feeling right now." I just looked at him.

"And you didn't look for her?" He nodded.

"I looked for before I came by here. I'd never want anything bad to happen to her. You just have to know this. I do love your mama, it's just, all this just made me not want to love anymore." I shook my head.

"And who's fault is that?" My phone buzzed and it was Marcus. He shouldn't be calling me back this fast. I picked up the phone and answered it.

"Sup– y-yo man calm d-down." I listened intently and what he just told me made me want to break down, but I wasn't about to let that happen.

"What you mean she's missing! Come get me now and did you find out where he is?!" I yelled into the phone and I took some meds and downed it with water.

"How did he even get her at her own home? Just come get me." I was ready for his ass this was going way too far.

Just as long as my baby wasn't in any danger anymore.

***

Melina

The bright light shined in my face. I was trying to move but that wasn't working. I opened my eyes fully and I was tied down to a chair.

I looked around and I was in my house. When and how did I get here?

A door opening and closing behind me made me try and turn around to see who it was. It could not have been my brother.

"M, I told you to stay out of this and follow my rules. Now, you gotta' go like Denise." I looked at him and spat at his feet.

"You disgust me! You know my son is coming for your head!" I shouted. He nodded and smiled.

"That's exactly why I have you now. He can't choose between his mom or his girl. Who do you think he'll choose? My goons are on the hunt for her right now. Remember I always win." He smiled and I tried desperately to get free.

"You don't always win! You sadistic bastard! I hate you." He shrugged and toyed with that sick ass knife.

"The feeling is mutual." He walked over to me and poked me with the knife. "So, I suggest you shut up before you really make me angry!" I screamed in pain and tried to wiggle free.

"You will not continue to control me!" I head butted him and watched as blood trickled down his nose. His whole demeanor change, he dropped the knife and balled up his fist. He struck me in the face twice I looked up at him with a bloody smile.

"Is that all you got bitch?" I continued to wiggle my hands. I raised my leg and kicked him in the balls. "It's over for your ass!" He laid there groaning in pain as he tried to get back up.

"Hit me if you're bad!" I screamed continuing to wiggle my fist. After I felt blood dripping from my wrist along with the burning sensation, I ripped my tied wrist free and I jumped up. I began to stomp on him, and I picked up his knife.

I stopped when I heard that cry of Alexus. "Keep hitting me or she and her baby dies!" He yelled as one of his guys held Alexus by her hair and wrist.

"Let her go, Richard! She has nothing to do with this!" I yelled. He started laughing as he got up and slapped me causing me to fall down the the floor.

"Move bitch! Move. I dare you too! If she's with Troy, then she has everything to do with this!" He shouted. I clung to his knife.

"He's coming to kill your ass!" I took the knife and stabbed him in the leg. He yelled out in pain and he tried to kick me again. I grabbed his leg and pushed him down.

I grabbed his gun and pointed it at the man. "Let her go!" I yelled.

"Melina! Don't do it, they have Ciara too!" I kept a good grip and pointed it at Richie.

"She's telling the truth. If you kill him, the other girl dies. This is a lose, lose situation." I sighed and lowered the gun.

"If I don't kill your ass, my son will. You weren't my brother anymore after what you did to Denise, still won't fix what the fuck you did! You can't bring her back, you caused this. And now look at you? Another death on your hands That's why Stephen is dead." His face dropped and he slapped me hard knocking me out.

Chapter Twenty-Seven
Troy

Riding in the car with Marcus, my heart raced uncontrollably. Usually I'd be zoned out when we had to go handle some shit. But this had me on an edge I could not bring my self back from. I was checking my guns for bullets. I couldn't believe what was going down right now. I was having the worse feeling ever. I could just feel death was coming.

One was for my mom, the other was for my baby and I couldn't fight this feeling anymore. "Marcus, can you call Lex? I'm having this horrible feeling. I need to hear her voice right now." He nodded and pulled out his phone. I stuffed the gun in the back of my pants and looked out the window.

"She ain't picking up." He mumbled. I looked at him then his phone, listening to her voicemail play.

"T-try again." He nodded and pressed her contact again. My leg began to ache, but I ignored it.

"Straight to voicemail dawg." He said once again, I tried so hard to stay calm, but as much as I tried, worrying was the only thing on my mind. My heart almost jumped out of my chest. When his phone rang, it was Lex. "Hand me the phone." He nodded and passed it over to me as he looked at the road.

I pressed the green button and began to speak. "Lex, baby you okay over there?" My smiled faded once I heard his voice.

"Bitch nigga! This ain't yo' girl. If you want her to live, I suggest you follow my instructions very fucking carefully. Her and your mama are in my care. Remember that." The line went dead, and I stared at the phone. The car came to a halt and Marcus looked at me with worry look once again.

"What's the matter? Is she okay?" I shook my head fighting my tears as I punched the dashboard.

"They got her to man! They got my girl!" I said biting my bottom lip in rage. He turned to me and immediately cocked his gun.

"We need to go get them, NOW!" I shook my head.

Monet Dragun

"He said if I don't follow HIS DAMN instructions, they are going to kill them. I can't lose Alexus, let alone my mom." Marcus had put his hand on my shoulder and patted it.

"We..." he was cut off by his phone ringing. I picked it up hearing Lex, cry and scream over the phone.

"L-let her go man! Let them go! This is b-between me and y-you." I said beyond pissed, and my jaw didn't even cause me pain.

"Nah, I think I may keep her and your baby. Turn ya' daughter or son into my little slaves." He said chuckling. "And do that thang over and over again. Maybe torture your bitch ass mom a little before I kill her."

"You listen and you listen good. You put one hand on my girl, or my momma and I swear, your death gon' be slow and painful! Keep fucking with me!" I shouted into the phone. He chuckled again and I could hear Lex scream for dear life and then Melina.

"I'll kill them right now! Keep on talking that shit and they'll be dead and gon'. I want my muthafucking my money! Yo pops owe me! I want you dead, but this will have to do for now." The phone line went dead, and I just stared at the pitchblack road.

"We're going in now!?" Marcus almost yelled. He was locked and loaded. He was ready to kill. He was my true brother. I nodded and pulled on my black skull cap. I made sure I had my other gun on me.

"One love." I held out my fist and he dapped it up.

"One love, bro." he pulled down his black skull cap and we got out of the car. I pushed the pain away and was focused to the point where I couldn't feel the pain. Marcus jogged up to the back door of the house. He twisted on his silencer, as I did mine as well. He shot at the door frame and kicked the door down. Richie's boys jumped up out of surprised and we shot them at first glance. I limped over to one of the guys laying on the floor while he was chocking up blood.

"Where Richie at!" He smiled at me and I shot him, moving on to the next. Me and Marcus moved on to the next rooms and they were empty.

"Clear. Wait? Did you hear that?" Marcus asked as we stood on the hard wood floors. We were still in Melina's house. The men on the ground were moaning and groaning.

"I said shut up!" We heard Richie's deep voice yell.

"My son knows I'm here. He's going to kill your weak ass."
POW!

Marcus immediately ran up the stairs softly and I was behind him. We could hear their voices as my mom's cries rang out.

"You're my sister, and you you do this shit to me? Betrayal is a bitch, ain't it!" I opened the door with my gun raised.

"You shot my momma?! HUH! You make one move and I swear I'm blowing yo' damn head off." He smiled and his shots rang off, and so did mine and Marcus'. I was way past done with letting him let out another breath.

I don't know what happened, but all I heard was yelling and screaming then the worse.

Monet Dragun

Chapter Twenty-Eight
Troy

"You shot my momma?! HUH! You make one move and I swear I'm blowing yo' damn head off." He smiled and his shots rang off, and so did mine and Marcus'. Richie had managed to shoot Marcus in the leg, but my man didn't go down. I was way past done with letting this snake take another breath. It was me or him at this point. We could hear more footsteps stomping up the steps.

I was about to fire another shot when I heard screaming coming from Alexus. Marcus covered me with raining bullets as more screams erupted from the love of my life. My eyes scanned the room and finally landed on her. Riche was ducking and diving as a man was wrestling over a gun with Alexus. She managed to win the fight and slide backwards as she shot the man wounding him in the shoulder, but she didn't have enough time to react as Riche stood a few feet from her. I tried to call out her name, but it was too late. Two single shots popped off as my eyes grew big at the sight before me.

It was like slow motion as I looked from Richie and watched my mother dive in front of Lex. He was trying so hard to kill Lex, and take the last person who really truly loved and gave a damn about me, but in the process, he shot my mom, his own sister. A couple more shots popped as Richie groaned in pain while he immediately grabbed his wound.

"Yeah nigga!" Marcus chanted as he reloaded his gun.

"Oh my God, Troy!" Lex cried out as she held my mom. Blood gargled from her mouth as her body trembled. I looked around at the terrible aftermath. I looked down at my mom. She had dove over Lex to cover her from the gun fire and here I was. I couldn't protect neither of them.

Richie was laying there with blood running out of his mouth shaking with his eyes heavy. This is not how this was supposed to go down. I could've lost my girl, best friend, and more importantly my own mother. I felt bad about how the shit went down. If I

Monet Dragun

didn't fire back, my boy would've been dead. But, my mom, she wasn't moving. She was motionless.

"Mama?" I said limping over to Alexus and her. She just laid there without a word to say. Marcus stood up over Richie and aimed his gun at his head.

"W-wait! I need to know if my mom is okay." He nodded in response, then kicked Richie's gun away from him all while he still held the gun over his head.

"Mama, move talk to me. Talk to me please." Lex still held her with tears.

"Baby, go sit over there please. You need to relax and just let me tend to her." My mom's hand fell onto my shoulder and I looked down at her. Lex moved and let me hold my mom. She was trying so hard to breath. It just made my heart melt. I didn't even get the chance to get to know her well enough yet.

"Baby, i-it's okay. It's everyone's time to go. I've escaped death once, but I can't beat him this time. My time on this earth is over son. My time is now. I just wish we had more time with one another." She broke out into a rapid cough and this was just breaking my heart even more.

"Mom, don't say that. It's not your time to go yet! Don't leave me. I need you ma' I'm sorry for all the bad things I said and..." her shaking hand came up and touched my face ever so gently.

"Don't you worry. Your mama made her mistakes. I've sinned, and I left you. That's the biggest regret of my life. I made my peace with God and you. Just know everything will be fine. I love you, my son." I was trying to be strong and then she took her last breath. I just stared down on her. I couldn't believe this was happening. I can't believe my real mom is gone. For good.

"Is she dead?! Oh my God!" Lex said holding me. I didn't say a word I just got up, but before I did, I kissed my mom's forehead and closed her eyes. I walked over to Marcus and asked for his gun.

He passed it over to me and I looked down on Richie who still had that grim look on his face. "Wipe that shit off your face! My mom, your sister is dead! Nigga any last words?" He just started to laugh, then broke into a harsh cough as blood spat out.

"This is not a motherfuck'in game, motherfucker. This is not a motherfucking game. Why you playin' man?" He started laughing, and I did a little too.

"Just know, you ain't bout this life." I smirked at him and looked at Marcus.

"I know." I cocked the gun and his smiled finally faded.

Pow! Pow!

I felt off two rounds and my aim was on point. The bullet hit right between his eyes and chest. He was lifeless.

"That was for my two moms, Melina and Denise Griffin." I tossed the gun to the side of him and walked back over to my grieving girlfriend.

"She didn't deserve that! Troy, he was trying to kill me, and she protected me. She protected me." I just pulled her into me, as she cried. Marcus limped over to me as he dialed something into his phone.

"This mess gon' get cleaned up and we gon' take your mom to her resting place. I'm sorry." I just nodded.

"She was a God-fearing woman. She didn't deserve that. You can't even trust your own blood." We walked out if the house to the truck.

"So, we gon' burn the house and make it look as if it was him that did it?" I nodded and rocked Lex back and forth in my arms as she cried into my white tee.

"I'm out this biz' just like I promised, baby. This baby has changed my life. Hell, this night has. Almost losing you damn near broke me. We gotta move on from this. My father got a lot of secrets out there that I know nothing about. I gotta make my moms proud. I can't live this life no more. Okay, Lex?" She sniffed into my chest and nodded.

"I love you and my baby. I'm not going a damn place you heard me."

"Yes, Troy, but she died protecting me. I can never forget that. I feel like it's my fault." I pecked her lips.

"Don't say that. Melina died because of her cold brother and she couldn't have me broken without you. She died for love, not because of you. She faced you, the baby, and me and I thank God for that. I thank God I found my momma. I love her with all my heart. I have to be strong for you and myself. They are looking over us as I speak. I just have to repent my sins. This life for me is no more. What about you, Marcus?" He stopped at a red light and nodded. He wrapped the cloth around his wound and tightened it.

"Yeah blood, I hear you. What you're saying is facts. I need to take care of my daughter. We brothers for life. Remember that." We dapped up and drove off to the hospital.

I don't know if I was okay, but I know I have to be strong about this. I just know his payback is over and done with. I just wished I didn't have to lose Melina in the process. I can't believe my momma died in my arms. It just wasn't fair.

***

Two weeks later

"We pray to the Lord that he takes Melina into your open arms. These innocent souls were taken by men with no fear in you, Lord.

Take her to the great pearly gates and watch over her. In the name of Jesus, we pray, amen." I stood there with a stone-cold look on my face. I stood there in my black army suit, hat and all. Everyone around me were crying and mourning my mother's death — even my father. But he was layered. His soul was black, and his heart was cold. I knew for sure he didn't care about her. It would be another woman to replace her soon. I noticed a young woman wrapped around his arm. She looked cleaned up, but I knew a woman like that. She was a street girl dress in all black to fool the ones around her. He didn't hold her like you'd hold your woman.

He held her like she needed help and searching for answers, just like me. My eyes stayed glued on them as his patted her shoulder as she cried. I watched his lips move. My father looked up from her and his eyes landed on me. I know he could see the fire in my eyes. Another one of his secrets was about to come out.

Me on the other hand, I knew it would come down to this. I was going to do everything in my power to find to do the right thing and take care of my responsibilities. I was never going to trust the enemy again. I made the mistake in trusting my enemy once.

As the pastor got done praying, the rain continued to pour. I clutched onto the roses, the very red and white roses that my mom once loved so much. I walked up the the casket and placed them on top of them. "I love you. I'll see you soon." I planted a kiss on there casket and walked away. I looked at all the people crying and raising their hands to God. My dad tried to talk to me, but everything was blocked out. Every noise, every cry, everything was out of my mind. I just wanted to be in peace with Lex and move on from this day and my past. Marcus held his head up as he looks at me.

"Brother's for life."

***

Marcus

"Shit baby, that hurts!" I groaned as Ciara stitched up my wound that had reopened from being to rough.

"Stay still. This wouldn't happen if you would be more careful Marcus. I have one more to do. I have to sterilize it again." I groaned and laid back on my stomach.

I got prepared for her to pour that shit on my leg. "Relax okay?" I nodded and took a deep breath. She poured it on and I was in damn agony.

"Baby, I'm all done now." She wrapped the new bandaging around my leg and she laid in my back. "Are you okay?" She questioned. I shook my head knowing damn well what I seen today was so sad.

"Troy's mom died two weeks ago ain't no way my brother is in the right mind set. After all the shit he's been through" I said lowly. She turned my face to hers a little.

"What?! I'm so sorry I couldn't be there. What happened? Is Troy okay?" She said with strain in her voice.

"It's a long story babe. And, yeah, I think he is, but truthfully, he's not, I know for a fact Troy is faking like everything is cool. He lost Denise and Melina, plus his dad doesn't make it any better, that old man knows more that what he leads Troy to believe, he ain't nothing but the damn devil. I know for a fact that old bastard got secrets that will further tear Troy apart. I don't know what to think of this no more. All I know is we out the game and that's on my dead homies." She kissed my forehead.

"He'll make it through this, I know he'll be okay, but I have something to tell you." She got off me and looked me in the eyes.

"Yeah? What is it?" She sighed.

"My business is going global and they want me to move away from Tennessee. Like New York, Cali, or Milan even." I looked at her with a happy face. "And I think I may be pregnant again." My eyes widen and she placed my hand on her stomach. "I want us all to move away from this shit hole. No man left behind." I smiled at her and kissed her deeply.

"This is why I love you. Plus, this is perfect. Troy will be a legit business owner and all." She paused. I looked at her face and cupped her chin.

"Babe, continue. What's on your mind?"

"It's just one more thing?" She said to me.

"What is it?" I questioned as Ciara let out a deep breath.

"I want my own gun. I want to learn how to shoot. You never know, you know?" I nodded and she kissed me.

"Yeah, you never know." I looked at her and kissed her forehead. "But you won't need it because all that bad shit is over with. I promise. I love you, baby." She looked at me and planted a soft off on my lips. I knew our lives were going to be better now. As Ciara snuggled up next to me on the couch there was a slight knock on the door.

"Ciara, go get the door ma. My side is fucking killing me." It was quiet as I continued watching this Netflix movie.

"Ciara?" I said shaking her slightly. Snoring erupted from her cause me to laugh.

"Yo, you gone pull the fake sleep move on ya boy. Damn. Ima get your ass back when you gotta change that baby diaper." I could see a smile creep on her face. I shook my head as I moved her body off me, I winced slightly as I got up. Honestly, I'm glad we out the game. I got a whole baby to live out here for. Slowly making my way to the door, the knock got a little harder and louder.

"Hold on! Fuck!" I shouted as I manuvered to the door and looked through the peephole, nothing. Frowning my brows, I could feel something wasn't right. So, I eased back from the door trying to get to the gun that was under the bench, but it was too late. The door flew open off the hinges and the last thing I saw was smoke, ski mask, and bullets. I lay on the ground gasping for air as blood dripped from my mouth into a pool of blood beside my head. I could hear a deep voices echo in my ear as I drifted in and out of consciousness.

"Yeah nigga… you thought this shit was over?"
POW!

To Be Continued…But First

184

Monet Dragun

"Is it done?" I asked him while standing outside of The PVall3y, the hottest strip club in the damn city. The owner had the best grand opening in business history. But G stood there counting the money like I just hadn't done that right in his face. This was the last payment I owed his boss. Messing with a loan shark ain't no joke. I paid my dues that's all that mattered now.

G looked up at me as his fingers shifted through the money quickly. On the last flick of this thumb, he said, "Fifty thousand dollars paid and full. You good to go but remember everything you worked for comes with a price. Have a good one. You better hope Troy don't come after yo ass. If you kept yo tracks clear, then nigga you're good. God I'm yo savior. Man, since that's the only thing you cared bout was destroying his life. You sure did that shit. Or is it?" G said, his words so icy, so rememberable.

I couldn't help but squint my eyes as he slid the money into the yellow envelope, sealed it, and then stuck it in his pocket, all while looking at me. I sighed once more as I looked down Burberry street. My dream was now coming to life. I couldn't believe I made it this far, but I wasn't done yet. This was the only step in ruining Troy. I still had some ways to go. G on the other hand, snapped his fingers in my face and said one last thing to me before walking away.

"Your debt is paid, but remember, Messiah is the king and you're just a pawn on the chessboard. If all goes to play, Troy will be out the picture. You may have paid this debt, but did you forget you sold your soul too? That, you can't never get back. Peace." G said as he walked backwards with a smirk. Then slowly turned around making his way towards his Benz as he whistled.

Sins can never be repented after you killed a man. That's a one-way ticket to hell and once I killed Troy Griffin, I was going to enjoy my eternal damnation.

Submission Guideline

Submit the first three chapters of your completed manuscript to ldpsubmissions@gmail.com, subject line: Your book's title. The manuscript must be in a .doc file and sent as an attachment. Document should be in Times New Roman, double spaced and in size 12 font. Also, provide your synopsis and full contact information. If sending multiple submissions, they must each be in a separate email.

Have a story but no way to send it electronically? You can still submit to LDP/Ca$h Presents. Send in the first three chapters, written or typed, of your completed manuscript to:

LDP: Submissions Dept
Po Box 944
Stockbridge, Ga 30281

DO NOT send original manuscript. Must be a duplicate.

Provide your synopsis and a cover letter containing your full contact information.

Thanks for considering LDP and Ca$h Presents.

Coming Soon from Lock Down Publications/Ca$h Presents

BOW DOWN TO MY GANGSTA

By **Ca$h**

TORN BETWEEN TWO

By **Coffee**

THE STREETS STAINED MY SOUL **II**

By **Marcellus Allen**

BLOOD OF A BOSS **VI**

SHADOWS OF THE GAME II

By **Askari**

LOYAL TO THE GAME **IV**

By **T.J. & Jelissa**

A DOPEBOY'S PRAYER **II**

By **Eddie "Wolf" Lee**

IF LOVING YOU IS WRONG… **III**

By **Jelissa**

TRUE SAVAGE **VII**

MIDNIGHT CARTEL III

DOPE BOY MAGIC IV

CITY OF KINGZ II

By **Chris Green**

BLAST FOR ME **III**

A SAVAGE DOPEBOY III

CUTTHROAT MAFIA III

By **Ghost**

A HUSTLER'S DECEIT III

Monet Dragun

KILL ZONE **II**

BAE BELONGS TO ME III

A DOPE BOY'S QUEEN III

By **Aryanna**

COKE KINGS V

KING OF THE TRAP II

By **T.J. Edwards**

GORILLAZ IN THE BAY V

De'Kari

THE STREETS ARE CALLING II

Duquie Wilson

KINGPIN KILLAZ IV

STREET KINGS III

PAID IN BLOOD III

CARTEL KILLAZ IV

DOPE GODS III

Hood Rich

SINS OF A HUSTLA II

ASAD

KINGZ OF THE GAME V

Playa Ray

SLAUGHTER GANG IV

RUTHLESS HEART IV

By Willie Slaughter

THE HEART OF A SAVAGE III

By Jibril Williams

FUK SHYT II

Sins of a Thug

By Blakk Diamond
THE REALEST KILLAZ III
By Tranay Adams
TRAP GOD III
By Troublesome
YAYO IV
A SHOOTER'S AMBITION III
By S. Allen
GHOST MOB
Stilloan Robinson
KINGPIN DREAMS III
By Paper Boi Rari
CREAM II
By Yolanda Moore
SON OF A DOPE FIEND III
By Renta
FOREVER GANGSTA II
GLOCKS ON SATIN SHEETS III
By Adrian Dulan
LOYALTY AIN'T PROMISED II
By Keith Williams
THE PRICE YOU PAY FOR LOVE II
By Destiny Skai
CONFESSIONS OF A GANGSTA II
By Nicholas Lock
I'M NOTHING WITHOUT HIS LOVE II
SINS OF A THUG II

By Monet Dragun
LIFE OF A SAVAGE IV
A GANGSTA'S QUR'AN II
MURDA SEASON II
GANGLAND CARTEL II
By **Romell Tukes**
QUIET MONEY III
THUG LIFE II
By **Trai'Quan**
THE STREETS MADE ME III
By **Larry D. Wright**
THE ULTIMATE SACRIFICE VI
IF YOU CROSS ME ONCE II
ANGEL III
By **Anthony Fields**
THE LIFE OF A HOOD STAR
By Ca$h & Rashia Wilson
FRIEND OR FOE II
By **Mimi**
SAVAGE STORMS II
By **Meesha**
BLOOD ON THE MONEY II
By J-Blunt
THE STREETS WILL NEVER CLOSE II
By K'ajji
NIGHTMARES OF A HUSTLA II
By King Dream

Sins of a Thug

KING OF NEW YORK I II,III IV V

RISE TO POWER I II III

COKE KINGS I II III IV

BORN HEARTLESS I II III IV

KING OF THE TRAP

By **T.J. Edwards**

IF LOVING HIM IS WRONG…I & II

LOVE ME EVEN WHEN IT HURTS I II III

By **Jelissa**

WHEN THE STREETS CLAP BACK I & II III

THE HEART OF A SAVAGE I II

By **Jibril Williams**

A DISTINGUISHED THUG STOLE MY HEART I II & III

LOVE SHOULDN'T HURT I II III IV

RENEGADE BOYS I II III IV

PAID IN KARMA I II III

SAVAGE STORMS

By **Meesha**

A GANGSTER'S CODE I &, II III

A GANGSTER'S SYN I II III

THE SAVAGE LIFE I II III

CHAINED TO THE STREETS I II III

BLOOD ON THE MONEY

By **J-Blunt**

PUSH IT TO THE LIMIT

By **Bre' Hayes**

BLOOD OF A BOSS **I, II, III, IV, V**

Sins of a Thug

SHADOWS OF THE GAME
By **Askari**
THE STREETS BLEED MURDER **I, II & III**
THE HEART OF A GANGSTA I II& III
By **Jerry Jackson**
CUM FOR ME I II III IV V
An **LDP Erotica Collaboration**
BRIDE OF A HUSTLA **I II & II**
THE FETTI GIRLS **I, II& III**
CORRUPTED BY A GANGSTA I, II III, IV
BLINDED BY HIS LOVE
THE PRICE YOU PAY FOR LOVE
DOPE GIRL MAGIC I II III
By **Destiny Skai**
WHEN A GOOD GIRL GOES BAD
By **Adrienne**
THE COST OF LOYALTY I II III
By Kweli
A GANGSTER'S REVENGE **I II III & IV**
THE BOSS MAN'S DAUGHTERS I II III IV V
A SAVAGE LOVE **I & II**
BAE BELONGS TO ME I II
A HUSTLER'S DECEIT I, II, III
WHAT BAD BITCHES DO I, II, III
SOUL OF A MONSTER I II III
KILL ZONE
A DOPE BOY'S QUEEN I II

194

Monet Dragun

By **Aryanna**
A KINGPIN'S AMBITON
A KINGPIN'S AMBITION **II**
I MURDER FOR THE DOUGH
By **Ambitious**
TRUE SAVAGE I II III IV V VI
DOPE BOY MAGIC I, II, III
MIDNIGHT CARTEL I II
CITY OF KINGZ
By **Chris Green**
A DOPEBOY'S PRAYER
By **Eddie "Wolf" Lee**
THE KING CARTEL **I, II & III**
By **Frank Gresham**
THESE NIGGAS AIN'T LOYAL **I, II & III**
By **Nikki Tee**
GANGSTA SHYT **I II &III**
By **CATO**
THE ULTIMATE BETRAYAL
By **Phoenix**
BOSS'N UP **I , II & III**
By **Royal Nicole**
I LOVE YOU TO DEATH
By Destiny J
I RIDE FOR MY HITTA
I STILL RIDE FOR MY HITTA
By **Misty Holt**

LOVE & CHASIN' PAPER

By **Qay Crockett**

TO DIE IN VAIN

SINS OF A HUSTLA

By **ASAD**

BROOKLYN HUSTLAZ

By **Boogsy Morina**

BROOKLYN ON LOCK I & II

By **Sonovia**

GANGSTA CITY

By **Teddy Duke**

A DRUG KING AND HIS DIAMOND I & II III

A DOPEMAN'S RICHES

HER MAN, MINE'S TOO I, II

CASH MONEY HO'S

By Nicole Goosby

TRAPHOUSE KING **I II & III**

KINGPIN KILLAZ I II III

STREET KINGS I II

PAID IN BLOOD **I II**

CARTEL KILLAZ I II III

DOPE GODS I II

By **Hood Rich**

LIPSTICK KILLAH **I, II, III**

CRIME OF PASSION I II & III

FRIEND OR FOE

By **Mimi**

Monet Dragun

STEADY MOBBN' **I, II, III**
THE STREETS STAINED MY SOUL
By **Marcellus Allen**
WHO SHOT YA **I, II, III**
SON OF A DOPE FIEND I II
Renta
GORILLAZ IN THE BAY **I II III IV**
TEARS OF A GANGSTA I II
DE'KARI
TRIGGADALE I II III
Elijah R. Freeman
GOD BLESS THE TRAPPERS I, II, III
THESE SCANDALOUS STREETS I, II, III
FEAR MY GANGSTA I, II, III IV, V
THESE STREETS DON'T LOVE NOBODY I, II
BURY ME A G I, II, III, IV, V
A GANGSTA'S EMPIRE I, II, III, IV
THE DOPEMAN'S BODYGAURD I II
THE REALEST KILLAZ I II
Tranay Adams
THE STREETS ARE CALLING
Duquie Wilson
MARRIED TO A BOSS… I II III
By Destiny Skai & Chris Green
KINGZ OF THE GAME I II III IV
Playa Ray
SLAUGHTER GANG I II III

197

RUTHLESS HEART I II III

By Willie Slaughter

FUK SHYT

By Blakk Diamond

DON'T F#CK WITH MY HEART I II

By Linnea

ADDICTED TO THE DRAMA I II III

By Jamila

YAYO I II III

A SHOOTER'S AMBITION I II

By S. Allen

TRAP GOD I II

By Troublesome

FOREVER GANGSTA

GLOCKS ON SATIN SHEETS I II

By Adrian Dulan

TOE TAGZ I II III

By Ah'Million

KINGPIN DREAMS I II

By Paper Boi Rari

CONFESSIONS OF A GANGSTA

By Nicholas Lock

I'M NOTHING WITHOUT HIS LOVE

SINS OF A THUG

By Monet Dragun

CAUGHT UP IN THE LIFE I II III

By Robert Baptiste

Monet Dragun

NEW TO THE GAME I II III
By **Malik D. Rice**
LIFE OF A SAVAGE I II III
A GANGSTA'S QUR'AN
MURDA SEASON
GANGLAND CARTEL
By **Romell Tukes**
LOYALTY AIN'T PROMISED
By Keith Williams
QUIET MONEY I II
THUG LIFE
By **Trai'Quan**
THE STREETS MADE ME I II
By **Larry D. Wright**
THE ULTIMATE SACRIFICE I, II, III, IV, V
KHADIFI
IF YOU CROSS ME ONCE
ANGEL I II
By **Anthony Fields**
THE LIFE OF A HOOD STAR
By Ca$h & Rashia Wilson
THE STREETS WILL NEVER CLOSE
By K'ajji
CREAM
By Yolanda Moore
NIGHTMARES OF A HUSTLA
By King Dream

<u>BOOKS BY LDP'S CEO, CA$H</u>

<u>TRUST IN NO MAN</u>
<u>TRUST IN NO MAN 2</u>
<u>TRUST IN NO MAN 3</u>
<u>BONDED BY BLOOD</u>
<u>SHORTY GOT A THUG</u>
<u>THUGS CRY</u>
<u>THUGS CRY 2</u>
<u>THUGS CRY 3</u>
<u>TRUST NO BITCH</u>
<u>TRUST NO BITCH 2</u>
<u>TRUST NO BITCH 3</u>
<u>TIL MY CASKET DROPS</u>
<u>RESTRAINING ORDER</u>
<u>RESTRAINING ORDER 2</u>
<u>IN LOVE WITH A CONVICT</u>
<u>LIFE OF A HOOD STAR</u>

<u>Coming Soon</u>
BONDED BY BLOOD 2
BOW DOWN TO MY GANGSTA

Monet Dragun

9 781952 936524